THE
CONFESSION
OF BROTHER
HALUIN

ELLIS PETERS

THE CONFESSION OF BROTHER HALUIN

THE CADFAEL CHRONICLES XV

Brother
CADFAEL

press
élan

A GENERAL PUBLISHING IMPRINT

First published in Great Britain by Headline in 1988
This edition published in Canada in 1995 by
élan press, an imprint of General Publishing Co. Limited
30 Lesmill Road, Toronto, Canada, M3B 2T6

Copyright © Ellis Peters 1988

CIP data available upon request from the
National Library of Canada.

ISBN 1-55144-100-4

Printed and bound in Great Britain by
Clays Ltd, St. Ives plc

THE
CONFESSION
OF BROTHER
HALUIN

The Journey of Brother

HALES

HARGEDON

To Shrewsbury

Forester's
Lodge

N

The route   Roads

Haluin and Brother Cadfael

R. Tame

ELFORD

VIVERS

FAREWELL

CHENET

LICHFIELD

Woodland

0 Miles 4

DJC

Chapter One

HE WORST of the winter came early, that year of 1142. After the prolonged autumn of mild, moist, elegiac days, December came in with heavy skies and dark, brief days that sagged upon the rooftrees and lay like oppressive hands upon the heart. In the scriptorium there was barely light enough at noon to form the letters, and the colours could not be used with any certainty, since the unrelenting and untimely dusk sapped all their brightness.

The weather-wise had predicted heavy snows, and in mid-month they came, not with blizzard winds, but in a blinding, silent fall that continued for several days and nights, smoothing out every undulation, blanching all colour out of the world, burying the sheep in the hills and the hovels in the valleys, smothering all sound, climbing every wall, turning roofs into ranges of white, impassable mountains, and the very air between earth and sky into an opaque, drifting whirl-pool of flakes large as lilies. When the fall finally ceased, and the heavy swags of cloud lifted, the Foregate lay half buried, so nearly smoothed out into one white level that there were scarcely any shadows except where the tall buildings of the abbey soared out of the pure pallor, and the eerie, reflected light made day even of night, where only a week before the ominous gloom had made night of day.

These December snows, which covered most of the west, did more than disrupt the lives of country people, starve some isolated hamlets, bury not a few hill shepherds with their flocks, and freeze all travel into enforced stillness; they overturned the fortunes of war, made sport of the preoccupations of princes, and sent history spinning off-course into the new year of 1143.

They also brought about a strange cycle of events in the abbey of Saint Peter and Saint Paul, at Shrewsbury.

In the five years that King Stephen and his cousin, the Empress Maud, had fought for the throne of England, fortune had swung between them like a pendulum many times, presenting the cup of victory to each in erratic turn, only to snatch it away again untasted, and offer it tantalisingly to the other contender. Now, in the white disguise of winter, it chose to turn probability topsy-turvy once again, and deliver the empress out of the king's mailed hands as by a miracle, just as his fist seemed closing securely on his prisoner, and his warfare triumphantly ending. Back to the beginning of the five-year struggle, and all to do again. But that was in Oxford, far away beyond the impassable snows, and some time would elapse before the news reached Shrewsbury.

What was happening in the abbey of Saint Peter and Saint Paul was no more than a small annoyance by comparison, or seemed so at first. An envoy from the bishop, lodged in one of the upper chambers of the guest-hall, and already irritated and displeased at being halted here perforce until the roads were passable again, was unpleasantly awakened in the night by the sudden descent of a stream of icy water on to his head, and made very sure that everyone within range of his powerful voice should hear of it without delay. Brother Denis the hospitaller made haste

8

to placate him, and move him to a dry bed elsewhere, but within the hour it became clear that while the first drenching soon slackened, a steady drip continued, and was soon joined by half a dozen more, spanning a circle some yards across. The great weight of snow on the southern roof of the guest-hall had somehow worked a passage through the lead and filtered in between the slates, perhaps even caved in a number of them. Pockets of the driven snow had felt the comparative warmth within, and with the mute malice of inanimate things had chosen to baptise the bishop's emissary. And the leak was rapidly getting worse.

There was urgent conference at chapter that morning over what should and could be done. Perilous and unpleasant work on roofs was certainly to be avoided if possible during such weather, but on the other hand, if repairs were delayed until the thaw came they were in for a flood, and the damage, limited at this point, might be greatly aggravated.

There were several among the brothers who had worked on the building of additions to the enclave, barns and stabling and storehouses, and Brother Conradin, who was still in his fifties and robust as a bull, had been one of the first child oblates, and worked as a boy under the monks of Seez, brought over by the founding earl to supervise the building of his abbey. Where the fabric was concerned, Brother Conradin's advice carried the greatest weight, and having viewed the extent of the leak in the guest-hall, he stated firmly that they could not afford to wait, or they might have to replace half the southern slope of the roof. They had timber, they had slates, they had lead. That southern slope overhung the drainage channel drawn off from the mill leat, frozen hard at present, but there would be no great difficulty in raising a scaffolding. True, it would be bitterly cold work up there, shifting the mountain of snow first, to ease away the deforming weight, and then replacing broken or displaced slates and repairing the lead flashings.

9

But if they worked in short spells, and were allowed a fire in the warming room all day as long as the work lasted, the job could be done.

Abbot Radulfus listened, nodded his formidable head with his usual prompt comprehension and decision, and said: 'Very well, do it!'

As soon as the long snowfall ceased, and the skies lifted, the tough inhabitants of the Foregate sallied forth from their houses, well muffled and armed with shovels and brooms and long-handled rakes, and began to clear their way out to the highroad, and between them dig out a passage to the bridge and the town, where no doubt the stout burgesses within the walls were tackling the same seasonal enemy. The frost still held, and day by day fretted away mysteriously into the air the surface fringes of every drift, by infinitely slow degrees lessening the load. By the time a few of the main highways were again passable, and a few travellers, either foolhardy or having no choice, were laboriously riding them, Brother Conradin had his scaffolding up, his ladders securely braced up the slope of the roof, and all hands taking their turn aloft in the withering cold, cautiously shifting the great burden of snow, to get at the fractured lead and broken slates. A moraine of crumpled, untidy snow hills formed along the frozen drainage channel, and one unwary brother, who had failed to hear or heed the warning shout from above, was briefly buried by a minor avalanche, and had to be dug out hurriedly and despatched to the warming room to thaw out.

By then way was open between town and Foregate, and news, however hampered and slow its passage, could be carried from Winchester even to Shrewsbury in time to reach the castle garrison and the sheriff of the shire some days before Christmas.

Hugh Beringar came down from the town hotfoot to share it with Abbot Radulfus. In a country debilitated by five years of desultory civil war it behoved state and church to work closely together, and where sheriff and abbot were of like mind they could secure for their people a comparatively calm and orderly existence, and fend off the worst excesses of the times. Hugh was King Stephen's man, and held the shire for him loyally enough, but with even greater goodwill he held it for the folk who lived in it. He would welcome, and this autumn and winter had certainly been expecting, the king's triumph at last, but his chief preoccupation was to hand over to his lord a county relatively prosperous, contented and intact when the last battle was over.

He came looking for Brother Cadfael as soon as he had left the abbot's lodging, and found his friend busy stirring a bubbling pot over his brazier, in his workshop in the herb-garden. The inevitable coughs and colds of winter, the chilblained hands and heels, kept him busy replenishing the medicine cupboard in the infirmary, and thanks to the necessary brazier his timber workshop was somewhat warmer to work in than the carrels of the scriptorium.

Hugh came bursting in upon him in a gust of cold air and a wave of what was for him perceptible excitement, though its outward signs would have escaped anyone who knew him less well than Cadfael did. Only the crisp exasperation of his movements and the abruptness of his greeting caused Cadfael to cease his stirring and fix attentively on the young sheriff's face, the pointed brilliance of his black eyes and the little pulse in his cheek.

'It's all overturned!' said Hugh. 'All to do again from the beginning!' And whatever that meant, and Cadfael did not trouble to ask, since he was certainly about to be told, there was no saying whether exasperation and frustration were not outmatched in Hugh's voice and face by amused relief. He flung himself down on the bench against the timber wall, and dangled his hands between his knees in a gesture of helpless resignation.

11

'A courier got through from the south this morning,' he said, raising his eyes to his friend's attentive face. 'She's gone! Out of the trap, and fled away to join her brother at Wallingford. The king's lost his prize. Even when he has her between his hands he lets her slip through his fingers. I wonder, I wonder,' said Hugh, opening his eyes wide at a new thought, 'whether he did not turn a blind eye and let her go, when it came to the point! It would be like him. God knows he wanted her badly enough, but he may have taken fright when it came to puzzling what he could do with her when he had her. It's one question I'd love to ask him – but never shall!' he concluded with an oblique grin.

'Are you telling me,' asked Cadfael cautiously, eyeing him across the brazier, 'that the empress is escaped out of Oxford, after all? With the king's army all round her, and stores down to starvation level in the castle, from what we last heard? And how did even she contrive it? Tell me next she's grown wings and flown over the king's lines to Wallingford! She could hardly walk through his siege vallations on foot, even if she managed to get out of the castle unseen.'

'Ah, but she did, Cadfael! She did both! She got out of the castle unseen, and passed through some part at least of Stephen's lines. To the best they can guess, she must have been let down by a rope from the rear of the tower towards the river, she and two or three of her men with her. There could not have been more. They muffled themselves all in white to be invisible against the snow. Indeed by all accounts it was snowing then, to hide them the better. They crossed the river on the ice, and walked the six miles or so to Abingdon, for it was there they got horses to take them on to Wallingford. Give her her due, Cadfael, this is a rare woman. From all accounts there's no living with her when she's in high feather, but by God I can see how a man could follow her when she's down.'

'So she's back with FitzCount, after all,' said Cadfael on a long, marvelling breath. Barely a month ago it had seemed certain that the empress and her most faithful and devoted ally were irrevocably cut off from each other, and might never meet again in this world.

Ever since September the lady had been under close siege in Oxford castle, the king's armies drawn tightly round her, the town in his hands, and he content to sit back and starve out her battered garrison. And now, all in one bold bid and one snowy night, she was out of her chains, free to re-muster her forces and take up the fight again on equal terms. Surely there never had been such a king as Stephen for conjuring defeat out of victory. But it was a quality they shared, perhaps native to their blood, for the empress too, when she was gloriously installed in Westminister, and her coronation but a few days away, had borne herself so arrogantly and harshly towards the obstinate burgesses of her capital that they had risen in fury and driven her out. It seemed that as often as either of them got within touch of the crown fortune took fright at the prospect of being in the service of either, and hurriedly snatched the prize away.

'So after all,' said Cadfael more placidly, as he lifted his bubbling pot to the grid at the side of the brazier, to simmer in peace, 'at least Stephen has got rid of his problem. He need worry no longer what to do with her.'

'True,' agreed Hugh wryly, 'he'd never have had the iron in him to put her in chains, as she did to him when she had him prisoner after Lincoln, and she's proved it would take more than stone walls to hold her. I fancy he's been blinking the issue all these months, looking no further than the moment when he would force her surrender. He's eased of all the troubles that would have been no more than beginning the day he made her prisoner. Better, perhaps, if he could winnow away her hopes so far that she'd be forced to go back to Normandy. But we've come to know the lady

13

better,' he acknowledged ruefully. 'She never gives up.'

'And how has King Stephen stomached his loss?' asked Cadfael curiously.

'As I've come to expect of him by this time,' said Hugh, with resigned affection. 'As soon as the lady was well out of it, Oxford Castle surrendered to him. Without her, he'd lost interest in the rest of the starved rats within. Most men would have taken out their rage on the garrison. Once, as you'll remember all too well, he let himself be persuaded to take such a revenge, here at Shrewsbury, God knows against his nature. Never again! As like as not it was the memory of Shrewsbury that kept Oxford safe. He let them march out untouched, on condition they dispersed to their homes. He's left the castle well garrisoned and supplied for his own cause, and made off to Winchester with his brother the bishop, to keep Christmas. And he's sent to call all his midland sheriffs there to keep it with him. It's long since he was in these parts, no doubt he's anxious to look us over afresh, and make sure that all his defences hold fast.'

'Now?' said Cadfael, surprised. 'To Winchester? You'll never make the journey in time.'

'Yes, we shall. We have four days, and according to the courier the thaw's well forward, further south, and the roads clear. I'll be away tomorrow.'

'And leave Aline and your boy to keep the feast without you! And Giles just past his third birthday, too!' Hugh's son was a Christmas babe, and had entered the world in the most extreme of winters, in frost and snow and bitter gales. Cadfael was his godfather and most devoted admirer.

'Ah, Stephen won't keep us long,' said Hugh confidently. 'He needs us where he placed us, to keep an eye on his shire revenues. I shall be home by the year's end, if all goes well. But Aline will be glad if you could pay her a visit or two while I'm gone. Father Abbot won't grudge you leave now and then, and that long lad of yours – Winfrid, is it? – he's

14

getting handy enough with the salves and medicines to be left on his own for an hour or two.'

'Very gladly I'll mind your flock for you at home,' said Cadfael heartily, 'while you're strutting at court. But you'll be missed, all the same. What a turnabout this has been! Five years of it now, and nothing gained on either part. And with the new year, no doubt it must all begin again. All that effort and waste, and nothing is changed.'

'Oh, yes, there's something changed, for what it's worth!' Hugh uttered a brief bark of laughter. 'There's a new contender on the scene, Cadfael. Geoffrey could spare no more than a meagre handful of knights to his wife's aid, but he's sent her something it seems he can part with more willingly. Either that or, as may very well be true, he's taken Stephen's measure shrewdly enough to know past doubt what he dare wager in safety. He's sent over their son in his Uncle Robert's care, to see if the English will rally to him rather than to his mother. Henry Plantagenet, nine years old – or did they say ten? No more than that! Robert brought him to her at Wallingford. By this time I fancy the boy's been whisked away to Bristol or Gloucester, out of harm's way. But if Stephen laid hold of him, what could he do with him? As like as not put him on board ship at his own expense, and send him well guarded back to France.'

'Do you tell me so?' Cadfael's eyes had opened wide in astonishment and curiosity. 'So there's a new star on the horizon, is there? And starting young! It seems one soul at least has a blessed Christmas assured, with her liberty won, and her son in her arms again. His coming will give her heart, no question. But I doubt if he'll do much more for her cause.'

'Not yet!' said Hugh, with prophetic caution. 'We'll wait and see what his mettle is. With his mother's stomach and Geoffrey's wit he may give the king trouble enough in a few years' time. We'd best make better use of what time we have,

15

and see to it the boy goes back to Anjou and stays there, and best of all, takes his mother with him. I wish,' said Hugh fervently, rising with a sigh, 'Stephen's own son promised better, we'd have no need to fear what the empress's sprig may have to show.' He shook off present doubts with an impatient twitch of his lean shoulders. 'Well, I'll be off and make ready for the road. We'll be away at first light.'

Cadfael lifted his cooling pot aside to the earth floor, and went out with his friend through the walled stillness of the herb-garden, where all his small, neat beds slept warmly through the frosts under deep snow. As soon as they let themselves out on to the path that skirted the frozen pools they could see distantly, beyond the glassy surface and the broad gardens on the northern side, the long slope of the guest-hall roof overhanging the drainage channel, the dark timber cage of scaffolding and ladders, and the two muffled figures working on the uncovered slates.

'I see you have your troubles, too,' said Hugh.

'Who escapes them, in winter? It's the weight of the snow that's shifted the slates, broken some of them, and found a way through to douse the bishop's chaplain in his bed. If we left it till the thaw we'd have a flood, and far worse damage to repair.'

'And your master-builder reckons he can make it good, frost or no frost.' Hugh had recognised the brawny figure halfway up the long ladder, hefting a hodful of slates surely few of his younger labourers could have lifted. 'Bitter work up there, though,' said Hugh, eyeing the highest platform of the scaffolding, stacked with a great pile of slates, and the two diminutive figures moving with painful caution on the exposed roof.

'We take it in short spells, and there's a fire in the warming-room when we come down. We elders are excused the service, but most of us take a turn, barring the sick and infirm. It's fair, but I doubt if it pleases Conradin. It irks

16

him having foolhardy youngsters up there, and he'd just as soon work only the ones he's sure of, though I will say he keeps a close watch on them. If he sees any blanch at being up so high, he soon has them on solid earth again. We can't all have the head for it.'

'Have you been up there?' asked Hugh curiously.

'I did my stint yesterday, before the light began to fail. Short days are no help, but another week should see it finished.'

Hugh narrowed his eyes against a sudden brief lance of sunlight that reflected back dazzlingly from the crystalline whiteness. 'Who are those two up there now? Is that Brother Urien? The dark fellow? Who's the other one?'

'Brother Haluin.' The thin, alert figure was all but obscured by the jut of the scaffolding, but Cadfael had seen the pair climb the ladders barely an hour earlier.

'What, Anselm's best illuminator? How comes it you allow such abuse of an artist? He'll ruin his hands in this bitter cold. Small chance of him handling a fine brush for the next week or two, after grappling with slates.'

'Anselm would have begged him off,' Cadfael admitted, 'but Haluin would have none of it. No one would have grudged him the mercy, seeing how valuable his work is, but if there's a hair shirt anywhere within reach Haluin will claim it and wear it. A lifelong penitent, that lad, God knows for what imagined sins, for I never knew him so much as break a rule since he entered as a novice, and seeing he was no more than eighteen when he took his first vows, I doubt if he'd had time to do the world much harm up to then. But there are some born to do penance by nature. Maybe they lift the load for some of us who take it quite comfortably that we're humankind, and not angels. If the overflow from Haluin's penitence and piety washes off a few of my shortcomings, may it redound to him for credit in the accounting. And I shan't complain.'

It was too cold to linger very long in the deep snow, watching the cautious activities on the guest-hall roof. They resumed their passage through the gardens, skirting the frozen pools where Brother Simeon had chopped jagged holes to let in air to the fish below, and crossing the mill-leat that fed the ponds by the narrow plank bridge glazed over with a thin and treacherous crust of ice. Closer now, the piers of the scaffolding jutted from the south wall of the guest-hall across the drainage channel, and the workers on the roof were hidden from sight.

'I had him with me among the herbs as a novice, long ago,' said Cadfael as they threaded the snowy beds of the upper garden and emerged into the great court. 'Haluin, I mean. It was not long after I ended my own novitiate. I came in at past forty, and he barely turned eighteen. They sent him to me because he was lettered, and had the Latin at his finger-ends, and after three or four years I was still learning. He comes of a landed family, and would have inherited a good manor if he hadn't chosen the cloister. A cousin has it now. The boy had been put out to a noble household, as the custom is, and was clerk to his lord's estate, being uncommonly bright at learning and figuring. I often wondered why he changed course, but as every man within here knows, there's no questioning a vocation. It comes when it will, and there's no refusal.'

'It would have been simpler to plant the lad straight into the scriptorium, if he came in with so much learning,' said Hugh practically. 'I've seen some of his work, he'd be wasted on any other labour.'

'Ah, but his conscience would have him pass through every stage of the common apprenticeship before he came to rest. I had him for three years among the herbs, then he did two years more at the hospital of Saint Giles, among the sick and crippled, and two more labouring in the gardens at the Gaye, and helping with the sheep out at Rhydycroesau,

18

before he'd settle to do what we found he could do best. Even now, as you saw, he'll have no privilege because he has a delicate hand with the brushes and pens. If others must slither perilously on a snowy roof, so will be. A good fault, mind you,' admitted Cadfael, 'but he takes it to extremes, and the Rule disapproves extremes.'

They crossed the great court towards the gatehouse, where Hugh's horse was tethered, the tall, raw-boned grey that was always his favourite mount, and could have carried twice or three times his master's light weight.

'There'll be no more snow tonight,' said Cadfael, eyeing the veiled sky and sniffing the light, languid wind, 'nor for a few days more, I fancy. Nor hard frost, either, we're on the edge of it. I pray you'll have a tolerable ride south.'

'We'll be away at dawn. And back, God willing, by the new year.' Hugh gathered his bridle and swung himself into the high saddle. 'May the thaw hold off until your roof's weatherproof again! And don't forget Aline will be expecting you.'

He was off out of the gate, with a sharp echo of hooves ringing from the cobbles, and a single brilliant spark that had come and gone almost before the iron shoe left the frozen ground. Cadfael turned back to the door of the infirmary, and went to check the stores in Brother Edmund's medicine cupboard. Another hour, and the light would be already dimming, in these shortest days of the year. Brother Urien and Brother Haluin would be the last pair up on the roof for this day.

Exactly how it happened no one ever clearly established. Brother Urien, who had obeyed Brother Conradin's order to come down as soon as the call came, pieced together what he thought the most probable account, but even he admitted there could be no certainty. Conradin, accustomed to being obeyed, and sensibly concluding that no one in his right senses would wish to linger a moment longer than he must in the bitter cold, had simply shouted his command, and turned away to clear the last of the day's broken slates out of the way of his descending workmen. Brother Urien let himself down thankfully to the boards of the scaffolding, and fumbled his way carefully down the long ladder to the ground, only too happy to leave the work. He was strong and willing, and had no special skills but a wealth of hard experience, and what he did would be well done, but he saw no need to do more than was asked of him. He drew off some yards to look up at what had been accomplished, and saw Brother Haluin, instead of descending the short ladder braced up the slope of the roof on his side, mount several rungs higher, and lean out sidelong to clear away a further sweep of snow and extend the range of the uncovered slates. It appeared that he had seen reason to suspect that the damage extended further on that side, and wished to sweep away the snow there to remove its weight and prevent worse harm.

The rounded bank of snow shifted, slid down in great folds upon itself, and fell, partly upon the end of the planks and the stack of slates waiting there, partly over the edge and sheer to the ground below. No such avalanche had been intended, but the frozen mass loosed its hold of the steep slates and dropped away in one solid block, to shatter as it struck the scaffolding. Haluin had leaned too far. The ladder slid with the snow that had helped to keep it stable, and he fell rather before than with it, struck the end of the planks a glancing blow, and crashed down without a cry to the frozen channel below. Ladder and snowfall dropped upon the planks and hurled them after him in a great down-pour of heavy, sharp-edged slates, slashing into his flesh.

Brother Conradin, busy almost beneath his scaffolding, had leaped clear only just in time, spattered and stung and half-blinded for a moment by the blown drift of the fall.

Brother Urien, standing well back, and arrested in the very act of calling up to his companion to stop, for the light was too far gone, uttered instead a great cry of warning, too late to save, and sprang forward, to be half-buried by the edge of the fall. Shaking off snow, they reached Brother Haluin together.

It was Brother Urien who came in haste and grim silence looking for Cadfael, while Conradin ran out the other way into the great court, and sent the first brother he encountered to fetch Brother Edmund the infirmarer. Cadfael was in his workshop, just turfing over his brazier for the night, when Urien erupted into the doorway, a dark, dour man burning with ill news.

'Brother, come quickly! Brother Haluin has fallen from the roof!'

Cadfael, no less sparing of words, swung about, clouted down the last turf, and reached for a woollen blanket from the shelf.

'Dead?' The drop must be forty feet at least, timber by way of obstacles on the way down, and packed ice below, but if by chance he had fallen into deep snow made deeper still by the clearance of the roof, he might yet be lucky.

'There's breath in him. But for how long? Conradin's gone for more helpers, Edmund knows by now.'

'Come!' said Cadfael, and was out of the door and running for the little bridge over the leat, only to change his mind and dart along the narrow neck of causeway between the abbey pools, and leap the leat at the end of it, to come the more quickly to where Haluin lay. From the great court the gleam of two torches advanced to meet them, and Brother Edmund with a couple of helpers and a hand-litter, hard on Brother Conradin's heels.

Brother Haluin, buried to the knees under heavy slates, with blood staining the ice beneath his head, lay still in the middle of the turmoil he had caused.

Chapter Two

HATEVER the risks of moving him, to leave him where he was for a moment longer than was necessary would have been to consent to and abet the death that already had a fast hold on him. In mute and purposeful haste they lifted aside the fallen planks and dug out with their hands the knife-edged slates that crushed and lacerated his feet and ankles into a pulp of blood and bone. He was far gone from them, and felt nothing that was done to him as they eased him out of the icy bed of the drain enough to get slings under him, and hoisted him on to the litter. In mourne procession they bore him out through the darkened gardens to the infirmary, where Brother Edmund had prepared a bed for him in a small cell apart from the old and infirm who spent their last years there.

'He cannot live,' said Edmund, looking down at the remote and pallid face.

So Cadfael thought, too. So did they all. But still there was breath in him, even if it was a harsh, groaning breath that spoke of head injuries perhaps past mending; and they went to work on him as on one who could and must live, even against their own virtual certainty that he could not.

23

With infinite, wincing care they stripped him of his icy garments, and padded him round with blankets wrapped about heated stones, while Cadfael went over him gently for broken bones, and set and bound the left forearm that grated as he handled it, and still brought never a flicker to the motionless face. He felt carefully about Haluin's head before cleaning and dressing the bleeding wound, but could not determine whether the skull was fractured. The bitter, snoring breathing indicated that it was, but be could not be sure. As for the broken feet and ankles, Cadfael laboured over them for a long time after they had covered the rest of Brother Haluin with warmed brychans against simple death of cold, his body laid straight and shored securely every way to guard against the shock and pain of movement should he regain his senses. As no one believed he would, unless it was an obstinate, secret remnant of belief that caused them so to exert themselves to nourish even the failing spark.

'He will never walk again,' said Brother Edmund, shuddering at the shattered feet Cadfael was laboriously bathing.

'Never without aid,' Cadfael agreed sombrely. 'Never on these.' But for all that he went on patiently putting together again, as best he could, the mangled remains.

Long, narrow, elegant feet Brother Haluin had had, in keeping with his slender build. The deep and savage cuts the slates had made penetrated to the bone in places, here and there had splintered the bone. It took a long time to clean away the bloody fragments, and bind up each foot at least into its human shape, and encase it in a hastily improvised cradle of felt, well padded within, to hold it still and let it heal as near as possible to what it had once been. If, of course, there was to be healing.

And all the while Brother Haluin lay snoring painfully and oblivious of all that was done to him, very far sunk beneath the lights and shadows of the world, until even his breathing subsided gradually into a mere shallow whisper, no more than the stirring of a solitary leaf in a scarcely perceptible breeze, and they thought that he was gone. But the leaf continued to stir, however faintly.

'If he comes to himself, even for a moment, call me at once,' said Abbot Radulfus, and left them to their watch.

Brother Edmund was gone to get some sleep. Cadfael shared the night watch with Brother Rhun, newest and youngest among the choir monks. One on either side of the bed, they stared steadily upon the unbroken sleep beyond sleep of a body anointed and blessed and armed for death.

It was many years since Haluin had passed out of Cadfael's care to go to manual labour in the Gaye. Cadfael re-examined with deep attention lineaments he had almost forgotten in their early detail, and found now both changed and poignantly familiar. Not a big man, Brother Haluin, but somewhat taller than the middle height, with long, fine, shapely bones, and more sinew and less flesh on them now than when first he came into the cloister, a boy still short of his full growth, and just hardening into manhood. Thirty-five or thirty-six he must be now, barely eighteen then, with the softness and bloom still on him. His face was a long oval, the bones of cheek and jaw strong and clear, the thin, arched brows almost black, shades darker than the mane of crisp brown hair he had sacrificed to the tonsure. The face upturned now from the pillow was blanched to a clay-white pallor, the hollows of the cheeks and deep pits of the closed eyes blue as shadows in the snow, and round the drawn lips the same livid blueness was gathering even as they watched. In the small hours of the night, when the life sinks to its frailest, he would end or mend.

Across the bed Brother Rhun knelt, attentive, unintimidated by another's death any more than he would be, some day, by his own. Even in the dimness of this small, stony room Rhun's radiant fairness, his face creamy with

25

youth, his ring of flaxen hair and aquamarine eyes, diffused a lambent brightness. Only someone of Rhun's virgin certainty could sit serenely by a deathbed, with such ardent loving-kindness and yet no taint of pity. Cadfael had seen other young creatures come to the cloister with something of the same charmed faith, only to see it threatened, dulled and corroded gradually by the sheer burden of being human under the erosion of the years. That would never happen to Rhun. Saint Winifred, who had bestowed on him the physical perfection he had lacked, would not suffer the gift to be marred by any maiming of his spirit.

The night passed slowly, with no perceptible change in Brother Haluin's unrelenting stillness. It was towards dawn when at last Rhun said softly: 'Look, he is stirring!'

The faintest quiver had passed over the livid face, the dark brows drew together, the eyelids tightened with the first distant awareness of pain, the lips lengthened in a brief grimace of stress and alarm. They waited for what seemed a long while, unable to do more than wipe the moist forehead, and the trickle of spittle that oozed from the corner of the drawn mouth.

In the first dim, reflected snow-light before dawn Brother Haluin opened his eyes, onyx-black in their blue hollows, and moved his lips to emit a hair-fine thread of a voice that Rhun had to stoop his young, sharp ear to catch and interpret.

'Confession . . .' said the whisper from the threshold between life and death, and for a while that was all.

'Go and bring Father Abbot,' said Cadfael.

Rhun departed silently and swiftly. Haluin lay gathering his senses, and by the growing clarity and sharpening focus of his eyes he knew where he was and who sat beside him, and was mustering what life and wit remained to him for a purpose. Cadfael saw the quickening of pain in the strained whiteness of mouth and jaw, and made to trickle a little of

26

the draught of poppies between his patient's lips, but Haluin kept them tightly clenched and turned his head away. He wanted nothing to dull or hamper his senses, not yet, not until he had got out of him what he had to say.

'Father Abbot is coming,' said Cadfael, close to the pillow. 'Wait, and speak but once.'

Abbot Radulfus was at the door by then, stooping under the low lintel. He took the stool Rhun had vacated, and leaned down to the injured man. Rhun had remained without, ready to run errands if he should be needed, and had drawn the door closed between. Cadfael rose to withdraw likewise, and suddenly yellow sparks of anxiety flared in Haluin's hollow eyes, and a brief convulsion went through his body and fetched a moan of pain, as though he had willed to lift a hand to arrest Cadfael's going, but could not do it. The abbot leaned closer, to be seen as well as heard.

'I am here, my son. I am listening. What is it troubles you?'

Haluin drew in breath, hoarding it to have a voice to speak with. 'I have sins . . .' he said, '. . . never told.' The words came slowly and with much labour, but clearly. 'One against Cadfael . . . Long past . . . never confessed . . .'

The abbot looked up at Cadfael across the bed. 'Stay! He wishes it.' And to Haluin, touching the lax hand that was too weak to be lifted: 'Speak as you can, we shall be listening. Spare many words, we can read between.'

'My vows,' said the thread-fine voice remotely. 'Impure . . . not out of devotion . . . Despair!'

'Many have entered for wrong reasons,' said the abbot, 'and remained for the right ones. Certainly in the four years of my abbacy here I have found no fault in your true service. On this head have no fear. God may have brought you into the cloister roundabout for his own good reasons.'

'I served de Clary at Hales,' said the thin voice. 'Better,

27

his lady – he being in the Holy Land then. His daughter . . .' A long silence while doggedly and patiently he renewed his endurance to deliver more and worse. 'I loved her . . . and was loved. But the mother . . . my suit was not welcome. What was forbidden us we took . . .'

Another and longer silence. The blue, sunken lids were lowered for a moment over the burning eyes. 'We lay together,' he said clearly. 'That sin I did confess, but never named her. The lady cast me out. Out of despair I came here . . . at least to do no more harm. And the worst harm yet to come!'

The abbot closed his hand firmly on the nerveless hand at Haluin's side, to hold him fast by the grip, for the face on the pillow had sunken into a mask of clay, and a long shudder passed through the bruised and broken body, and left it tensed and chill to the touch.

'Rest!' said Radulfus, close to the sufferer's ear. 'Take ease! God hears even what is not said.'

It seemed to Cadfael, watching, that Haluin's hand responded, however feeble its hold. He brought the drink of wine and herbs with which he had been moistening the patient's mouth while he lay senseless, and trickled a few drops between the parted lips, and for the first time the offering was accepted, and the strings of the lean throat made the effort to swallow. His time was not yet. Whatever more he might have to heave off his heart, there was yet time for it. They fed him sips of wine, and watched the clay of his features again cohere into flesh, however pale and feeble. This time, when he came back to them, it was very faintly and with eyes still closed.

'Father . . .?' questioned the remote voice fearfully.

'I am here. I will not leave you.'

'Her mother came . . . I did not know till then Bertrade was with child! The lady was in terror of her lord's anger when he came home. I served then with Brother Cadfael, I had learned . . . I knew the herbs . . . I stole and gave her . . . hyssop, fleur-de-luce . . . Cadfael knows better uses for them!'

Yes, better by far! But what could help a badly congested chest and a killing cough, in small doses, or fight off the jaundice that turned a man yellow, could also put an end to the carrying of a child, in an obscene misuse abhorrent to the church and perilous even to the woman it was meant to deliver. From fear of an angry father, fear of shame before the world, fear of marriage prospects ruined and family feuds inflamed. Had the girl's mother entreated him, or had he persuaded her? Years of remorse and self-punishment had not exorcised the horror that still wrung his flesh and contorted his visage.

'They died,' he said, harsh and loud with pain. 'My love and the child, both. Her mother sent me word – dead and buried. A fever, they gave it out. Dead of a fever – nothing more to fear. My sin, my most grievous sin . . . God knows I am sorry!'

'Where true penitence is,' said Abbot Radulfus, 'God does surely know. Well, this grief is told. Have you done, or is there more yet to tell?'

'I have done,' said Brother Haluin. 'But to beg pardon. I ask it of God – and of Cadfael, that I abused his trust and his art. And of the lady of Hales, for the great grief I brought upon her.' Now that it was out he had better control of voice and words, the crippling tension was gone from his tongue, and weak though his utterance was, it was lucid and resigned. 'I would die cleansed and forgiven,' he said.

'Brother Cadfael will speak on his own behalf,' said the abbot. 'For God, I will speak as he gives me grace.'

'I forgive freely,' said Cadfael, choosing words with more than his accustomed care, 'whatever offence was done against my craft under great stress of mind. And that the means and the knowledge were there to tempt you, and I not

29

there to dissuade, this I take to myself as much as ever I can charge them to you. I wish you peace!'

What Abbot Radulfus had to say upon God's behalf took longer. There were some among the brothers, Cadfael thought, who would have been startled and incredulous if they could have heard, at finding their abbot's formidable austerity could also hold so much measured and authoritative tenderness. A lightened conscience and a clean death were what Haluin desired. It was too late to exact penance from a dying man, and deathbed comfort cannot be priced, only given freely.

'A broken and a contrite heart,' said Radulfus, 'is the only sacrifice required of you, and will not be despised.' And he gave absolution and the solemn blessing, and so left the sickroom, beckoning Cadfael with him. On Haluin's face the ease of gratitude had darkened again into the indifference of exhaustion, and the fires were dead in eyes dulled and half-closed between swoon and sleep.

In the outer room Rhun was waiting patiently, drawn somewhat aside to avoid hearing, even unwittingly, any word of that confession.

'Go in and sit with him,' said the abbot. 'He may sleep now, there will be no ill dreams. If there should be any change in him, fetch Brother Edmund. And if Brother Cadfael should be needed, send to my lodging for him.'

In the panelled parlour in the abbot's lodge they sat together, the only two people who would ever hear of the offence with which Haluin charged himself, or have the right in private to speak of his confession.

'I have been here only four years,' said Radulfus directly, 'and know nothing of the circumstances in which Haluin came here. It seems one of his earliest duties here was to help you among the herbs, and there he acquired this knowledge he put to such ill use. Is it certain this draught he concocted could kill? Or may this truly have been a death from fever?'

'If the girl's mother used it on her, she could hardly be mistaken,' said Cadfael ruefully. 'Yes, I've known hyssop to kill. I was foolish to keep it among my stores, there are other herbs that could take its place. But in small doses, both herb and root, dried and powdered, are excellent for the yellow distemper, and useful with horehound against chest troubles, though the blue-flowered kind is milder and better for that. I've known women use it to procure abortion, in great doses that purge to the extreme. Small wonder if sometimes the poor girl dies.'

'And this was surely during his novitiate, for he cannot have been here long if this child was his, as he supposes. He can have been only a boy.'

'Barely eighteen, and the girl surely no more, if as old. It is some extenuation,' said Cadfael firmly, 'if they were in the same household, seeing each other daily, of equal birth, for he comes of a good family, and as open to love as are most children. In fact,' said Cadfael, kindling, 'what I wonder at is that his suit should have been rejected out of hand. He was an only son, there was a good manor would have been his if he had not taken vows. And he was a very pleasing youth, as I recall, lettered and gifted. Many a knight would have welcomed him as a match for his daughter.'

'It may be her father already had other plans for her,' said Radulfus. 'He may have betrothed her to someone else in childhood. And her mother would hardly venture to countenance a match in her husband's absence, if she went in such awe of him.'

'She need not, however, have rejected the boy utterly. If she had let him hope he would have waited, surely, and not tried to force her hand by forestalling marriage. Though it may be I do him wrong there,' Cadfael relented. 'It was not calculation, I fancy, that brought him into the girl's bed, but

31

too rash affection. Haluin would never make a schemer.'

'Well, for better or worse,' said Radulfus with a weary sigh, 'it was done, and cannot be undone. He is not the first, and will not be the last young man to fall into that error, nor she the first nor the last poor child to suffer for it. At least she has kept her good name. Easy to see why he feared to confide, for her sake, even under the seal of confession. But it is all long ago, eighteen years, his age when it befell. Let us at least secure him a peaceful ending.'

It was the general view that a peaceful ending was the best that could be hoped for for Brother Haluin, and that prayers for him ought not to presume to look towards any other outcome, all the more as his brief return to his senses rapidly lapsed again into a deeper unconsciousness, and for seven days, while the festival of the Nativity came and passed, he lay oblivious of the comings and goings of his brethren round his bed, ate nothing, uttered no sound but the hardly perceptible flutter of his breath. Yet that breath, however faint, was steady and even, and as often as drops of honeyed wine were presented to his lips, they were accepted, and the cords of his throat moved of themselves, docilely swallowing, while the broad, chilly brow and closed eyes never by the least quiver or contraction revealed awareness of what his body did.

'As if only his body is here,' said Brother Edmund, soberly pondering, 'and his spirit gone elsewhere until the house is again furbished and clean and waiting to be lived in.'

A sound biblical analogy, Cadfael considered, for certainly Haluin had himself cast out the devils that inhabited him, and the dwelling they vacated might well lie empty for a while, all the more if there was to be that unlooked-for and improble act of healing, after all. For however this prolonged withdrawal might resemble dying, Brother

32

Haluin would not die. Then we had better keep a good watch, thought Cadfael, taking the parable to its fitting close, and make sure seven devils worse than the first never manage to get a foot in the door while he's absent. And prayers for Haluin continued with unremitting fervour throughout the festivities of Christmas and the solemn opening of the new year.

The thaw was beginning by that time, and even then it was a slow thaw, wearing away each day, by slow degrees, the heavy wastes of snow from the great fall. The work on the roof was finished without further mishap, the scaffolding taken down, and the guest-hall once again weatherproof. All that remained of the great upheaval was this still and silent witness in his isolated bed in the infirmary, declining either to live or die.

Then, in the night of the Epiphany, Brother Haluin opened his eyes and drew a long, slow breath like any other man awaking without alarm, and cast his wondering gaze round the narrow room until it rested upon Brother Cadfael, mute and attentive on the stool beside him.

'I am thirsty,' said Haluin trustingly, like a child, and lay passive on Cadfael's arm to drink.

They half expected him to sink again into his unconscious state, but he remained languid but aware all that day, and in the night his sleep was natural sleep, shallow but tranquil. After that he turned his face to life, and did not again look over his shoulder. Once risen from the semblance of death he came back to the territory of pain, and its signature was on his drawn brow and set lips, but he bore it without complaint. His broken arm had knitted while he lay ignorant of his injuries, and caused him only the irritating aches of healing wounds, and it seemed both to Cadfael and Edmund, after a day or two of keeping close watch on him, that whatever had been shaken out of place within his head had healed as the outer wound had healed, medicined by stillness and repose. For his mind was clear. He remembered the icy roof, he remembered his fall, and once when he was alone with Cadfael he showed that he recalled very clearly his confession, for he said after a long while of silent thought:

'I did shamefully by you, long ago, now you tend and medicine me, and I have made no amends.'

'I've asked none,' said Cadfael equably, and began with patient care to unfold the wrappings from one maimed foot, to renew the dressings he had been replacing night and morning all this time.

'But I need to pay all that is due. How else can I be clean?'

'You have made full confession,' said Cadfael reasonably, 'you have received absolution from Father Abbot himself, beware of asking more.'

'But I have done no penance. Absolution so cheaply won leaves me still a debtor,' said Haluin heavily.

Cadfael had laid bare the left foot, the worse mangled of the pair. The surface cuts and wounds had healed over, but what had happened to the labyrinth of small bones within could never be put right, they had fused into a misshapen clot, twisted and scarred, discoloured in angry dark reds and purples. Yet the seamed skin had knitted and covered all.

'If you have debts,' said Cadfael bluntly, 'they bid fair to be paid in pain to the day you die. You see this? You will never set this firmly to ground again. I doubt if you will ever walk again.'

'Yes,' said Haluin, staring out through the narrow chink of the window at the darkening wintry sky, 'yes, I shall walk. I will walk. If God allows, I will go on my own feet again, though I must borrow crutches to help them bear me. And if Father Abbot gives me his countenance, when I have learned to use what props are left to me I will go myself to Hales, to beg forgiveness of Adelais de Clary, and keep a night's vigil at Bertrade's tomb.'

34

In his own mind Cadfael doubted if either the dead or the living would take any great comfort from Haluin's fondly resolved atonement, or still be nursing any profound recollection of him, after eighteen years. But if the pious intent gave the lad courage and determination to live and labour and be fruitful again, why discourage him? So all he said was:

'Well, let's first mend all that can be mended, and put back some of that lost blood into you, for you'll get no leave to go anywhere as you are now.' And contemplating the right foot, which at least still bore some resemblance to a human foot, and had a perceptible and undamaged ankle-bone, he went on thoughtfully: 'We might make some sort of thick felt boots for you, well padded within. You might get one foot to the ground yet, though you'll need the crutches. Not yet – not yet, nor for weeks yet, more likely months. But we'll take your measure, and see what we can fashion between us.'

On reflection, Cadfael felt that it might be wise to warn Abbot Radulfus of the expiation Brother Haluin had in mind, and did so after chapter, in the privacy of the abbot's parlour.

'Once he had heaved the load off his heart,' said Cadfael simply, 'he would have died content if it had been his fortune to die. But he is going to live. His mind is clear, his will is strong, and if his body is meagre it's wiry enough, and now that he sees a life ahead of him he'll not be content to creep out of his sins by way of absolution without penance. If he was of a lighter mind, and could be coaxed to forget this resolve as he gets well, for my part I would not blame him, I'd be glad of it. But penitence without penance will never be enough for Haluin. I'll hold him back as long as I can, but trust me, we shall hear of this again, as soon as he feels able to attempt it.'

'I can hardly frown upon so fitting a wish,' said the abbot reasonably, 'but I can forbid it until he is fit to undertake it. If it will give him peace of mind I have no right to stand in his way. It may also be of some belated comfort to this unhappy lady whose daughter died so wretchedly. I am not familiar,' said Radulfus, pondering the proposed pilgrimage warily, 'with this manor of Hales, though I have heard the name of de Clary. Do you know where it lies?'

'Towards the eastern edge of the shire, Father, it must be a matter of twenty-five miles or so from Shrewsbury.'

'And this lord who was absent in the Holy Land – he can have been told nothing of the true manner of his daughter's death, if his lady went in such awe of him. It is many years past, but if he is still living this visit must not take place. It would be a very ill thing for Brother Haluin to salve his own soul by bringing further trouble and danger upon the lady of Hales. Whatever her errors, she has suffered for them.'

'For all I know, Father,' Cadfael admitted, 'they may both be dead some years since. I saw the place once, on the way from Lichfield on an errand for Abbot Heribert, but I know nothing of the household of de Clary.'

'Hugh Beringar will know,' said the abbot confidently. 'He has all the nobility of the shire at his finger-ends. When he returns from Winchester we may ask him. There's no haste. Even if Haluin must have his penance, it cannot be yet. He is not yet out of his bed.'

Chapter Three

UGH AND his escort came home four days after Epiphany. Much of the snow was gone by then, the weather grey, the days short and sombre, the nights hovering on the edge of frost, so that the thaw continued its gradual way, and there was no flooding. After such a heavy fall a rapid thaw would have seen a great mass of water coming down the river and draining from every drift, and the Severn would have backed up the Meole Brook and flooded the lower part of the fields, even if the enclave itself escaped inundation. This year they were spared that trouble, and Hugh, kicking off his boots and shrugging off his cloak in his own house by Saint Mary's church, with his wife bringing him his furred shoes and his son clinging to his sword-belt and clamouring to have his new, painted wooden knight duly admired, was able to report an easy journey for the time of year, and a satisfactory reception at court for his stewardship.

'Though I doubt if this Christmas truce will last long,' he said to Cadfael later, after acquainting the abbot with all the news from Winchester. 'He's swallowed the failure at Oxford gallantly enough, but for all that he's on his mettle for vengeance, he'll not sit still for long, winter or no. He wants Wareham back, but it's well stocked, and manned to the battlements, and Stephen never did have the patience for a siege. He'd like a fortress more to the west, to carry the war to Robert's country. There's no guessing what he'll try first. But he wants none of me or my men there in the south, he's far too wary of the earl of Chester to keep me long out of my shire. Thank God, for I'm of the same mind myself,' said Hugh blithely. 'And how have you been faring? Sorry I am to hear your best illuminator had a fall that all but ended him. Father Abbot told me of it. I can hardly have left you an hour, that day, when it happened. Is it true he's mending well?'

'Better than any of us ever expected,' said Cadfael, 'least of all the man himself, for he was certainly bent on clearing his soul for death. But he's out of the shadow, and in a day or two we'll have him out of his bed. But his feet are crippled for life, the slates chopped them piecemeal. Brother Luke is cutting some crutches to his measure. Hugh,' said Cadfael directly, ' what do you know of the de Clarys who hold the manor of Hales? There was one of them was a crusader nearly twenty years back. I never knew him, he was after my time in the east. Is he still living?'

'Bertrand de Clary,' said Hugh promptly, and looked up at his friend with quickening interest. 'What of him? He died years back, ten or more it must be. His son holds the honour now. I've had no dealings with them, Hales is the only manor they hold in this shire, the *caput* and most of their lands are in Staffordshire. Why, what's put de Clary in your mind?'

'Why, Haluin has. He was in their service before he took the cowl. It seems he feels he has left unpaid some debt he still owes in that direction. It came to mind when he made what he took to be his deathbed confession. In something he feels he offended, and has it on his conscience still.'

That was all that could be told, even to Hugh, the

confessional being sacred, and if nothing more was offered, Hugh would ask for nothing more, however he might speculate on what had not been said.

'He's set on making the journey to set the account straight, when he's fit to undertake it. I was wondering . . . If this Bertrand's widow is no longer in the land of the living, either, as well Haluin should know it at once, and put it out of his mind.'

Hugh was eyeing his friend with steady interest and a tolerant smile. 'And you want him to have nothing to trouble about, body or mind, but getting back into the way of living as soon as may be. I'm no help, Cadfael. The widow's living still. She's there at Hales, she paid her dues last Michaelmas. Her son's married to a Staffordshire wife, and has a young son to succeed him, and from all accounts his mother is not of a nature to share another woman's household without meddling. Hales is her favourite home, she keeps there from choice and leaves her son to rule his own roost, while she makes sure of ruling hers. No doubt it suits them both very well. I should not be even so well-informed,' he said by way of explanation, 'if we had not ridden some miles of the way from Winchester with a company of de Clary's men, dispersing from the siege of Oxford. The man himself I never saw, he was still delayed at court when we left. He'll be on his way home by now, unless Stephen keeps him for whatever move he has next in mind.'

Cadfael received this news philosophically but without pleasure. So she was still living, this woman who had sought to help her daughter to an abortion, and succeeded only in helping her to her death. Not the first nor the last to come by such a death. But what must the mother's despair and guilt have been then, and what bitter memories must remain even now, beneath the ashes of eighteen years? Better, surely, to let them lie buried still. But Haluin's self-torturing conscience and salvation-hungry soul had their rights, too. And after all, he had been just eighteen years old! The woman who had forbidden him any aspiration to her daughter's affection must have been double his age. She might, thought Cadfael almost indignantly, have had the wisdom to see how things began to be between those two, and taken steps to separate them in time.

'Did you ever feel, Hugh, that it might be better to let even ill alone,' wondered Cadfael ruefully, 'rather than let loose worse? Ah, well! He has not even tried his crutches yet. Who knows what changes a few weeks may bring.'

They lifted Brother Haluin out of his bed in the middle of January, found him a corner near the infirmary fire, since he could not move about freely like the others to combat the cold, and treated his body, stiff from long lying, with oil and massage to get the sinews working again. To occupy his hands and mind they brought him his colours and a little desk to work on, and gave him a simpler page to adorn until his fingers should regain their deftness and steadiness. His mangled feet had healed and fused into misshapen forms, and there was no question as yet of letting him attempt to stand on them, but Cadfael allowed him to try the crutches Brother Luke had made for him, with support on either side, to get accustomed to the heft and balance of them, and the shaped and padded props under his armpits. If neither foot could ever be brought to support him again, even the crutches would not be of any use, but both Cadfael and Edmund agreed that there was every hope of the right foot being restored to use in time, and even the left might eventually provide a grain of assistance, with a little ingenuity in shoeing the invalid.

To that end Cadfael called in, at the end of the month, young Philip Corviser, the provost's son, and they put their heads together over the problem, and between them produced a pair of boots as ill-matched in appearance as were the feet for which they were intended, but adapted as best they could devise to give strong support. They were of thick felt with a leather sole, built up well above the ankles and laced close with leather thongs to support and protect the damaged flesh and make full use of the shin-bones, which were intact. Philip was pleased with his work, but wary of praise until the boots were tried on, and found to be wearable without pain, and blessedly warm in this wintry weather.

And all that was done for him Brother Haluin accepted gratefully and humbly, and went on doggedly refreshing eye and hand with his reds and blues and delicately laid gold. But as often as the hours of leisure came round he would be precariously hoisting himself out of his corner bench with shoulders braced upon his crutches, poised to reach for the support of wall or bench if his balance was shaken. It took some time for the sinews to recover their toughness in his wasted legs, but early in February he could set his right foot firmly to the ground, and even stand on it briefly without other support, and from that time on he began to use his crutches in earnest, and to master them. He was seen again, dutiful and punctual, in his stall at chapter, and in the choir at every office. By the end of February he could even set the blocked toe of his left boot to the ground, to help hold him steady and secure on his crutches, though never again would that foot be able to support his weight, light though he was.

In one thing he was fortunate, that the winter, once that first early snowfall had thawed and vanished, was not a hard one. There were occasional spells of frost, but none that lasted long, and after January such snow-showers as there were were fitful and slight, and did not lie long. When he had his balance and was used to his new gait he could exercise his skills outdoors as well as in, and grew expert, fearful only of the cobbles of the court when they were glazed with frost.

At the beginning of March, with the days lengthening, and the first cautious and reluctant signs of spring in the air,

Brother Haluin rose in chapter, when all the urgent business of the day was over, and meekly but resolutely made a plea which only Abbot Radulfus and Brother Cadfael could fully understand.

'Father,' he said, his dark eyes fixed unwaveringly on the abbot's face, 'you know that in my trouble I conceived a desire to make a certain pilgrimage, if I should by God's grace be restored. Great mercy has been shown to me, and if you will give me leave, I wish now to register my vow in heaven. I beg your sanction and the prayers of my brothers that I may fulfil what I promise, and return in peace.'

Radulfus regarded the petitioner in silence for a disturbingly long time, his face revealing neither approval nor disapproval, though the fixity of his gaze brought a surge of blood into Haluin's hollow cheeks.

'Come to me after chapter,' said the abbot then, 'and I will hear what you intend, and judge whether you are yet fit to undertake it.'

In the abbot's parlour Haluin repeated his request in open terms, as to men before whom his spirit was naked and known. Cadfael knew why he himself had been summoned to attend. Two reasons, indeed, stood clear: he was the only other witness of Haluin's confession, and might therefore be admitted into his counsels; and he could speak as to Haluin's fitness to set out on such a journey. He had not yet guessed at a third reason, but he was not quite easy in his mind as he listened.

'I must not and will not hold you back,' said the abbot, 'from what is needful for your soul's health. But I think you ask too soon. You cannot yet have regained your strength. And it is not yet spring, however well we happen to have fared these last weeks. There may still be bitter weather to come. Think how recently you have been close to death, and spare putting yourself in such hardship until you are fitter to bear it.'

42

'Father,' said Haluin ardently, 'it is because I have been close to death that I must not delay. How if death should reach for me again before I can expiate my sin? I have seen how it can lay its hand on a man in a moment, in the twinkling of an eye. I have had my warning. I must heed it. If I die in paying the penance due from me, that I will embrace as fitting. But to die and not have made any amend, that would be endless reproach to me. Father,' he said, burning up like a stirred fire, 'I truly loved her, I loved her according to the way of marriage, I would have loved her lifelong. And I destroyed her. I have hidden my sins too long, now that I have confessed them I long to complete the atonement.'

'And have you thought of the miles you must go and return? Are you in any case to ride?

Haluin shook his head vigorously at that. 'Father, I have vowed already in my heart and will repeat the vow on the altar, to go on foot to the place where she is buried, and on foot return – on these feet that brought me to the earth and made me to face the truth of my unshriven offences. I can go, I have learned how the innocent lame must go. Why should not I, who am guilty of so much, suffer the same labours? I can endure it. Brother Cadfael knows!'

Brother Cadfael was none too pleased at being called in witness, and none too happy about saying anything which could promote this obsessed enterprise, but neither could he see any genuine peace of mind for this tormented creature until the expiation was completed.

'I do know he has the will and the courage,' he said. 'Whether he has the strength is another matter. And whether he has the right to force his body to the death in order to cleanse his soul is something on which I will not judge.'

Radulfus pondered for some minutes in sombre silence, eyeing the petitioner with a fixity which should have caused

43

him to stir uneasily and lower his gaze had there been anything false or pretentious in his purpose. But Haluin's wide, earnest eyes sustained the encounter ardently.

'Well, I acknowledge your desire to atone, late though it comes,' said the abbot at last, 'and I understand the better since the delay of years has not been for your own sake. Go, then, make the attempt. But I will not permit you to go alone. There must be someone with you in case you founder, and should that happen, you must allow him to make such dispositions for your safety as he sees fit. If you endure the journey well, he need not do anything to impair your sacrifice, but if you fall by the wayside, then he stands as my representative, and you must obey him as you obey me.'

'Father,' said Haluin in anxious protest, 'my sin is mine alone, my confession sealed and sacred. How can I let another man come so close, without myself breaking that seal? It would be a violation even to cause wonder and question concerning this penance of mine.'

'You shall have a companion who need neither wonder nor question,' said the abbot, 'since he already knows, at your own telling. Brother Cadfael shall come with you. His company and his prayers can only be of comfort and benefit to you. Your confidence and the lady's memory will be in no danger, and he is well qualified to care for you along the way.' And to Cadfael, turning, he said: 'Will you undertake this charge? I do not believe he is fit to go alone.'

Small choice, thought Cadfael, but not altogether displeased at the instruction, either. There was still, somewhere deep within him, a morsel of the *vagus* who had roamed the world from Wales to Jerusalem and back to Normandy for forty years before committing himself to stability within the cloister, and an expedition sanctioned, even ordered by authority could be welcomed as blessed, instead of evaded as a temptation.

'If you so wish, Father,' he said, 'I will.'

44

'This journey will take several days. I take it that Brother Winfrid will be competent to dispense whatever may be needed, with Edmund to guide him?'

'For a few days,' agreed Cadfael, 'they should manage well enough. I have stocked the infirmary cupboard only yesterday, and in the workshop there's a good supply of all the common remedies usually called for in the winter. Should something unforeseen be needed, Brother Oswin could come back from Saint Giles to help for a while.'

'Good! Then, son Haluin, you may prepare for this journey, and set out when you are ready, tomorrow if you will. But you will submit yourself to Brother Cadfael if your strength fails you, and do his bidding as faithfully as within these walls you have always done mine.'

'Father,' said Haluin fervently, 'I will.'

At the altar of Saint Winifred Brother Haluin recorded his solemn vow that same evening after Vespers, to leave himself no way out, with a white-faced vehemence which indicated to Cadfael, who witnessed it at Haluin's own wish, that this implacable penitent in his deepest heart knew and feared the labour and pain he was imposing on himself, and embraced it with a passion and resolution Cadfael would rather have seen devoted to a more practical and fruitful enterprise. For who would benefit by this journey, even though it passed successfully, except the penitent himself, at least partially restored to his self-respect? Certainly not the poor girl who had committed no worse sin than to venture too much for love, and who surely was long since in a state of grace. Nor the mother who must long ago have put this evil dream behind her, and must now be confronted by it once again after years. And Cadfael was not of the opinion that a man's main business in this world was to save his own soul. There are other ailing souls, as there are ailing bodies, in need of a hoist towards health.

But Haluin's needs were not his needs. Haluin's bitter years of silent self-blame certainly called for a remedy.

'On these most holy relics,' said Brother Haluin, with his palm pressed against the drapings that covered the reliquary, 'I record my penitential vow: that I will not rest until I have gone on foot to the tomb in which Bertrade de Clary lies, and there passed a night's vigil in prayer for her soul, and again on foot returned here to the place of my due service. And if I fail of this, may I live forsworn and die unforgiven.'

They set out after Prime, on the fourth morning of March, out at the gate and along the Foregate towards Saint Giles and the highroad due east. The day was cloudy and still, the air chill but not wintry cold. Cadfael viewed the way ahead in his mind, and found it not too intimidating. They would be leaving the western hills behind them, and with every mile eastward the country about them would subside peaceably into a green level. The road was dry, for there had been no recent rain, and the cloud cover above was high and pale, and threatened none, and there was a grassy verge such as could be found only on the king's highways, wide on either side the track, easy walking even for a crippled man. The first mile or two might pass without grief, but after that the constant labour would begin to tell. He would have to be the judge of when to call a halt, for Haluin was likely to grit his teeth and press on until he dropped. Somewhere under the Wrekin they would find a hospitable refuge for the night, for there were abbey tenants there among the cottagers, and any hut along the way would willingly give them a place by the fire for a midday rest. Food they had with them in the scrip Cadfael carried.

In the brisk hopefulness of morning, with Haluin's energy and eagerness at their best, they made good speed, and rested at noon very pleasurably with the parish priest at

Attingham. But in the afternoon the pace slowed somewhat, and the strain began to tell upon Haluin's hardworking shoulders, aching from the constant weight and endlessly repeated stress, and the cold as evening approached numbed his hands on the grips of his crutches, in spite of their mufflings of woollen cloth. Cadfael called a halt as soon as the light began to fade into the windless March dusk, grey and without distances, and turned aside into the village of Uppington, to beg a bed for the night at the manor.

Haluin had been understandably silent along the road, needing all his breath and all his resolution for the effort of walking. Fed and at ease in the evening, he sat watching Cadfael in accepting silence still for a while.

'Brother,' he said at last, 'I take it very kindly that you've come with me on this journey. With no other but you could I speak without conceal of that old grief, and before ever we see Shrewsbury again I may sorely need to speak of it. The worst of me you already know, and I will never say word in excuse. But in eighteen years I have never until now spoken her name aloud, and now to utter it is like food after starvation.'

'Speak or be silent as the need takes you,' said Cadfael, 'and I'll hear or be deaf according to your wish. But as for tonight you should take your rest, for you've come a good third part of the way, and tomorrow, I warn you, you'll find some aches and pains you knew nothing of, from labouring so hard and so long.'

'I am tired,' admitted Haluin, with a sudden and singularly touching smile, as brief as it was sweet. 'You think we cannot reach Hales tomorrow, then?'

'Don't think of it! No, we'll get as far as the Augustinian canons at Wombridge, and spend another night there. And you'll have done well to get so far in the time, so don't grudge the one day more.'

'As you think best,' said Haluin submissively, and lay

down to sleep with the confiding simplicity of a child charmed and protected by his prayers.

The next day was less kind, for there was a thin, spasmodic rain that stung at times with sleet, and a colder wind from the north-east, from which the long, green, craggy bulk of the Wrekin gave them no shelter as the road skirted it to the north. But they reached the priory before dusk, though Haluin's lips were fast clenched in determination by then, and the skin drawn tight and livid over his cheekbones with exhaustion, and Cadfael was glad to get him into the warmth, and go to work with oiled hands on the sinews of his arms and shoulders, and the thighs that had carried him so bravely all day long.

And the third day, early in the afternoon, they came to the manor of Hales.

The manor house lay a little aside from the village and the church, timber-built on a stone undercroft, in level, well-drained fields, with gentle wooded slopes beyond. Within its wooden fence stable and barn and bakehouse were ranged along the pale, well maintained and neat. Brother Haluin stood in the open gateway, and looked at the place of his old service with a face fixed and still, only his eyes alive and full of pain.

'Four years,' he said, 'I kept the manor roll here. Bertrand de Clary was my father's overlord, I was sent here before I was fourteen, to be page to his lady. Will you believe, the man himself I never saw, before I came here he was already in the Holy Land? This is but one of his manors, the only one in these parts, but his son was already installed in his place, and ruled the honour from Staffordshire. She always liked Hales best, she left her son to his lordship and settled here, and it was here I came. Better for her if I had never entered this house. Better far for Bertrade!'

'It's too late,' said Cadfael mildly, 'to do right whatever

was done amiss then. This day is for doing a right what you have pledged yourself to do now, and for that it is not too late. You'll be freer with her, maybe, if I wait for you without.'

'No,' said Haluin. 'Come with me! I need your witness, I know it will be just.'

A tow-haired youth came out of the stable with a pitchfork in his hands, steaming gently in the chill air. At sight of two black Benedictine habits in the gateway he turned and came towards them, leisurely and amiable.

'If you're wanting a bed and a meal, Brothers, come in, your cloth's always welcome here. There's good lying in the loft, and they'll feed you in the kitchen if you'll please to walk through.'

'I do remember,' said Haluin, his eyes still fixed upon a distant past, 'your lady kept always a hospitable house for travellers. But I shall need no bed this night. I have an errand to the lady Adelais de Clary herself, if she will give me audience. A few minutes of her time is all I ask.'

The boy shrugged, staring them over with grey, unreadable Saxon eyes, and waved them towards the stone steps that led up to the hall door.

'Go in and ask for her woman, Gerta, she'll see if the lady'll speak with you.' And he stood to watch them as they crossed the yard, before turning back to his labours among the horses.

A manservant was just coming up the steps from the kitchen into the passage as they entered the great doorway. He came to ask their business, and being told, sent off a kitchen boy to carry word to the lady's woman of the chamber, who presently came out from the hall to see who these monastic guests might be. A woman of about forty years, very brisk and neat, plain in her dress and plain in her face, for she was pock-marked. But of her confidence in office there was no question. She looked them over somewhat

49

superciliously, and listened to Haluin's meekly uttered request without a responsive smile, in no hurry to open a door of which she clearly felt herself the privileged custodian.

'From the abbey at Shrewsbury, you come? And on the lord abbot's business, I suppose?'

'On an errand the lord abbot has sanctioned,' said Haluin.

'It is not the same,' said Gerta sharply. 'What other than abbey business can send a monk of Shrewsbury here? If this is some matter of your own, let my lady know with whom she is dealing.'

'Tell her,' said Haluin patiently, leaning heavily on his crutches, and with eyes lowered from the woman's unwelcoming face, 'that Brother Haluin, a Benedictine monk of Shrewsbury abbey, humbly begs her of her grace to receive him.'

The name meant nothing to her. Clearly she had not been in Adelais de Clary's service, or certainly not in her confidence or even close enough to guess at her preoccupations, eighteen years ago. Some other woman, perhaps nearer her mistress's years, had filled this intimate office then. Close body-servants, grown into their mistress's trust and into their own blood-loyalty, carry a great treasury of secrets, often to their deaths. There must somewhere, Cadfael thought, watching in silence, be a woman who would have stiffened and opened her eyes wide at that name, even if she had not instantly known the changed and time-worn face.

'I will ask,' said the tirewoman, with a touch of condescension still, and went away through the hall to a leather-curtained doorway at the far end. Some minutes passed before she appeared again, drawing back the hangings, and without troubling to approach them, called from the doorway: 'My lady says you may come.'

The solar they entered was small and dim, for the windward of the two windows was shuttered fast against the weather, and the tapestries that draped the walls were old, and in rich dark colours. There was no fireplace, but a stone hearth laid close to the most sheltered corner carried a charcoal brazier, and between that and the one window that gave light a woman was sitting at a little embroidery frame, on a cushioned stool. Against the light from the window she showed as a tall, erect shape, dark-clothed, while the glow of the brazier shone in copper highlights on her shadowed face. She had left her needle thrust into the stretched cloth. Her hands were clenched fast on the raised arms of the stool, and her eyes were on the doorway, into which Brother Haluin lurched painfully on his crutches, his one serviceable foot sore with use and bearing him wincingly at every step, the blocked toe of his left foot barely touching the floor as a meagre aid to balance. Constant leaning into the crutches had hunched his shoulders and bent his straight back. Having heard his name, she must surely have expected something nearer to the lively, comely young man she had cast out all those years ago. What could she make now of this mangled wreckage?

He was barely within the room when she rose abruptly to her feet, stiff as a lance. Over their heads she spoke first to the waiting-woman, who had made to follow them in.

'Leave us!' said Adelais de Clary. And to Haluin, as the leather curtain swung heavily into place between solar and hall: 'What is this? What have they done to you?'

Chapter Four

HE MUST, Cadfael reckoned, growing used to the play of light and shadow within the room, be within ten years of his own age, but she looked younger. The dark hair that was coiled in heavy braids on either side of her head was barely touched with grey, and the imperious, fine bones of her face had kept their imperishable elegance though the flesh that covered them was a little shrunken and sapless now, and her body had grown angular and lean as the juices of youth dried up. Her hands, though shapely still, betrayed her with swollen knuckles and seamed veins, there was a languor upon her pale skin at throat and wrist where once the rounded gloss of youth had been. But for all that, in the oval face, the long, resolute lips and large eyes in their deep settings Cadfael saw the ashes of great beauty. No, not ashes, embers, still alive and as hot at least as the coals burning in the heart of the brazier.

'Come nearer!' she said. And when Haluin stood before her with the light upon his face, pale and cold light from the window, flushed from the fire: 'It is you!' she said. 'I wondered. How have you come to this?'

Her voice was low-pitched, full and authoritative, but the

first implication of dismay and concern was gone. She looked at him neither compassionately nor coldly, but with a kind of detached indifference, a curiosity of no deep root.

'This is no man's blame but mine,' said Haluin, 'Don't regard it! I have what I earned. I came by a great fall, but by the grace of God I am alive, who by this time had thought to be dead. And as I have eased my soul to God and my confessor for old sins, so I come to beg forgiveness of you.'

'Was that needful?' she said, marvelling. 'After so many years, and all this way?'

'Yes, it was needful. I do greatly need to hear you say that you forgive me the wrong I did, and the grief I brought upon you. There can be no rest for me now until the leaf is washed clear of every last stain.'

'And you have told over all the old writing,' said Adelais with some bitterness, 'all that was secret and shameful, have you? To your confessor! And how many more? This good brother who bears you company? The whole household at chapter? Could you not bear to be still a sinner unshriven, rather than betray my daughter's name to the world, and she so long in her grave? I would have gone sinful into purgatory rather!'

'And so would I!' cried Haluin, wrung. 'But no, it is not so. Brother Cadfael bears me company because he is the only one who knows, excepting only Abbot Radulfus, who heard my confession. No other will ever know from us. Brother Cadfael was also grossly wronged in what I did, he had a right to give or withhold forgiveness. It was from his store and after his teaching that I stole those medicines I gave to you.'

She turned her gaze upon Cadfael in a long, steady stare, and her face, for once seen clearly, was intent and still. 'Well,' she said, again turning away into indifference, 'it was very long ago. Who would remember now? And I am not dying yet. What do I know! I shall need a priest myself some day, I could better have answered you then. Well, to put an end to it . . . Have what you ask! I do forgive you. I would not add to what you suffer. Go back in peace to your cloister. I forgive you as I hope for forgiveness.'

It was said without passion; the brief spurt of anger was already gone. It cost her no effort to absolve him, she did it as neutrally, it seemed, and with as little feeling as she would have handed out food to a beggar. Of gentlewomen of her nobility alms could properly be asked, and granting was a form of largesse, the due fulfilment of a rite of lordship. But what she gave lightly came as relieving grace to Haluin. The braced tension went out of his leaning shoulders and stiffly clenched hands. He bent his head humbly before her, and uttered his thanks in a low and halting voice, like a man momentarily dazed.

'Madam, your mercy lifts a load from me, and from my heart I am grateful.'

'Go back to the life you have chosen and the duties you have undertaken,' she said, again seating herself, though she did not yet reach for her needle. 'Think no more of what happened long ago. You say you have a life spared. Use it as best you can, and so will I mine.'

It was dismissal, and as such Haluin accepted it. He made her a deep reverence, and turned carefully upon his crutches, and Cadfael reached a hand to steady him in the movement. She had not so much as bidden them be seated, perhaps too shaken by so sudden and startling a visit, but as they reached the doorway she called after them suddenly:

'Stay if you will, take rest and meat in my house. My servants will provide you everything you need.'

'I thank you,' said Haluin, 'but our leave of absence enjoins a return as soon as my pilgrimage here is done.'

'God hasten your way home, then,' said Adelais de Clary, and with a steady hand took up her needle again.

*   *   *

55

The church lay a short distance from the manor, where two tracks crossed, and the huddle of village house-plots gathered close about the churchyard wall.

'The tomb is within,' said Haluin, as they entered at the gate. 'It was never opened when I was here, but Bertrand's father is buried here, and surely it must have been opened for Bertrade. She died here. I am sorry, Cadfael, that I refused hospitality also for you, I had not thought in time. I shall need no bed tonight.'

'You said no word of that to the lady,' Cadfael observed.

'No. I hardly know why. When I saw her again my heart misgave me that I did ill to bring before her again that old pain, that the very sight of me was an offence to her. Yet she did forgive. I am the better for that, and she surely none the worse. But you could have slept easy tonight. No need for two to watch.'

'I'm better fitted for a night on my knees than you,' said Cadfael. 'And I am not sure the welcome there would have been very warm. She wished us gone. No, it's very well as it is. Mostly likely she thinks we're on the homeward way already, off her land and out of her life.'

Haluin halted for a second with his hand on the heavy iron ring latch of the church door, his face in shadow. The door swung open, creaking, and he gripped his crutches to ease himself down the two wide, shallow steps into the nave. It was dim and stonily chilly within. Cadfael waited a moment on the steps till his eyes grew accustomed to the changed light, but Haluin set off at once up the nave towards the altar. Nothing here was greatly changed in eighteen years, and nothing had been forgotten. Even the rough edges of the floor tiles were known to him. He turned aside towards the righthand wall, his crutches ringing hollowly, and Cadfael, following, found him standing beside a stone table-tomb fitted between the pillars. The carved image recumbent there was in crude chain-mail, and had

56

one leg crossed over the other, and a hand on his sword-hilt. Another crusader, surely the father of Bertrand, who in his turn had followed him to the Holy Land. This one, Cadfael calculated, might well have been with Robert of Normandy's army in my time, at the taking of Jerusalem. Clearly the de Clary men were proud of their warfare in the east.

A man came through from the sacristy, and seeing two unmistakable Benedictine habits, turned amicably to come towards them. A man of middle age, in a rusty black cassock, advancing upon them with a mildly enquiring expression and a welcoming smile. Haluin heard his steps, soft as they were, and swung about gladly to greet a remembered neighbour, only to recoil on the instant at seeing a stranger.

'Good day, Brothers! God be with you!' said the priest of Hales. 'To travellers of your cloth my house is always open, like this house of God. Have you come far?'

'From Shrewsbury,' said Haluin, strongly recovering himself. 'Forgive me, Father, if I was taken aback. I had expected to see Father Wulfnoth. Foolish of me, indeed, for I have not been here for many years, and he was growing grey when I knew him, but to me in youth it seemed he would be here for ever. Now I dare hardly ask!'

'Father Wulfnoth is gone to his rest,' said the priest, 'seven years ago now it must be. Ten years back I came here, after he was brought to his bed by a seizure, and three years I looked after him until he died. I was newly priest then, I learned much from Wulfnoth, his mind was clear and bright if the flesh had failed him.' His good-natured round face offered sympathetic curiosity. 'You know this church and this manor, then? Were you born in Hales?'

'No, not that. But for some years I served with the lady Adelais at the manor. Church and village I knew well, before I took the cowl at Shrewsbury. Now,' said Haluin earnestly, observing how brightly he was studied, and feeling the need to account for his return, 'I have good need to give thanks for escaping alive from a mishap that might have caused my death, and I have taken thought to discharge, while I may, every debt I have on my conscience. Of which number, one brings me here to this tomb. There was a lady of the de Clary family whom I reverenced, and she died untimely. I should like to spend the night here at her burial place, in prayers for her. It was long before your time, eighteen years ago now. It will not disturb you if I spend the night here within?'

'Why, as to that, you'd be welcome,' said the priest heartily, 'and I could light a cresset for you, it gives some help against the cold. But surely, Brother, you're under some mistake. True, what you say puts this before my time, but Father Wulfnoth told me much concerning the church and the manor, he'd been in the service of the lords of Hales all his life. It was they helped him to his studies and set him up here as priest. There has been no burial here in this tomb since the old lord died, this one who's carved here on the stone. And that was more than thirty years back, it's his grandson rules now. A lady of the family, you say? And died young?'

'A kinswoman,' said Haluin, low-voiced and shaken, his eyes lowered to the stone which had not been raised for thirty years. 'She died here at Hales, I had thought she must be buried here.' He would not name her, or betray more than he must of himself and what moved him, even to this kindly man. And Cadfael stood back from them, watched, and held his peace.

'And only eighteen years ago? Then be certain, Brother, she is not here. If you knew Father Wulfnoth, you know you can rely upon what he told me. And I know his wits were sharp until the day he died.'

'I do believe it,' said Haluin, quivering with the chill of disappointment. 'He would not be mistaken. So – she is not here!'

'But this is not the chief seat of the de Clary honour,' the

58

priest pointed out gently, 'for that's Elford, in Stafford-shire. The present lord Audemar took his father there for burial, the family has a great vault there. If there are any close kin dead these last years, that's where they'll be. No doubt the lady you speak of was also taken there to lie among her kinsfolk.'

Haluin seized upon the hope hungrily. 'Yes . . . yes, it could well be so, it must be so. There I shall find her.'

'I have no doubt of it,' said the priest. 'But it's a long way to go afoot.' He had sensed an urgency that was very unlikely to listen to reason, but he did his best to temper it. 'You'd be well advised to go mounted, if you must go now, or put it off for longer days and better weather. At least come within, to my house, and take meat with me, and rest overnight.'

But that Haluin would not do, so much was already clear to Brother Cadfael. Not while there was still an hour or more of daylight left at the windows, and he had still the strength to go a mile further. He excused himself with slightly guilty thanks, and took a restrained leave of the good man, who watched them in wondering speculation until they had climbed the steps to the porch, and closed the door after them.

'No!' said Cadfael firmly, as soon as they were clear of the churchyard, and passing along the track between the village houses to reach the highroad. 'That you cannot do!'

'I can, I must!' Brother Haluin responded with no less determination. 'Why should I not?'

'Because, in the first place, you do not know how far it is to Elford. As far again as we have come, and half as far after that. And you know very well how hard you have pushed yourself already. And in the second place, because you were given leave to attempt this journey in the belief that it would end here, and we two return from here. And so we should. No, never shake your head at me, you know very well Father Abbot never envisaged more than that, and would never have given you leave for more. We should turn back here.'

'How can I?' Haluin's voice was implacably reasonable, even tranquil. His way was perfectly clear to him, and he was patient with dissent. 'If I turn back, I am forsworn. I have not yet done what I vowed to do, I should go back self-condemned and contemptible. Father Abbot would not wish that, however little either he or I expected so long a penance. He gave me leave until I had accomplished what I swore to do. If he were here to be asked, he would tell me to go on. I said I would not rest until I had gone on foot to the tomb where Bertrade lies buried, and there passed a night in prayer and vigil, and that I have not done.'

'Through no fault of yours,' said Cadfael strenuously.

'Does that excuse me? It is a just judgement on me that I must go double the way. If I fail of this, I said, may I live forsworn and die unforgiven. On the blessed relics of Saint Winifred, who has been so good to us all, I swore it. How can I turn back? I would rather die on the road, at least still faithfully trying to redeem my vow, than abandon my faith and honour, and go back shamed.'

And who was that speaking, Cadfael wondered, the dutiful monk, or the son of a good Norman house, from a line at least as old as King William's when he came reaching for the crown of England, and without the irregularity of bastardy, at that. No doubt but pride is a sin, and unbecoming a Benedictine brother, but not so easily shed with the spurs and title of nobility.

Haluin, too, had caught the fleeting implication of arrogance, and flushed at the recognition, but would not draw back from it. He halted abruptly, swaying on his crutches, and detached a hand in haste to take Cadfael by the wrist. 'Don't chide me! Well I know you could, and your face shows me I deserve it, but spare to condemn. I can do no other. Oh, Cadfael, I do know every argument you could justly use against me, I have thought of them, I think of them still, but still I am bound. Bound by vows I will not, dare not break. Though my abbot judge me rebellious and disobedient, though my abbey cast me out, that I must bear. But to take back what I have pledged to Bertrade, that I will not bear.'

The flush of blood mantling in his pale cheeks became him, warmed away the faded look of emaciation from illness, and even stripped some years from him. In stillness he stood upright, stretching his bent back upward between the braced crutches. No persuasion was going to move him. As well accept it.

'But you, Cadfael,' he said, gripping the wrist he held, 'you have made no such vow, you are not bound. No need for you to go further, you have done all that was expected of you. Go back now, and speak for me to the lord abbot.'

'Son,' said Cadfael, between sympathy and exasperation, 'I am fettered as fast as you, and you should know it. My orders are to go with you in case you founder, and to take care of you if you do. You are on your own business, I am on the abbot's. If I cannot take you back with me I cannot go back.'

'But your work,' protested Haluin, dismayed but unwavering. 'Mine can well wait, but you'll be missed. How will they manage without you for so long?'

'As best they can. There's no man living who cannot be done without,' said Cadfael sturdily, 'and just as well, since there's a term to life for every man. No, say no more. If your mind's made up, so is mine. Where you go, I go. And since we have barely an hour of daylight left to us, and I fancy you have no wish to seek a bed here in Hales, we had better move gently on, and look for a shelter along the way.'

*   *   *

Adelais de Clary rose in the morning and went to Mass, as was her regular habit. She was meticulous in her religious observances and in almsgiving, keeping up the old custom of her husband's household. And if her charity seemed sometimes a little cold and distant, at least it was constant and reliable. Whenever the parish priest had a special case in need of relief, he brought it to her for remedy.

He walked with her to the gate after the office, dutiful in attendance. 'I had two Benedictines come visiting yester-day,' he said as she was drawing her cloak about her against a freshening March wind. 'Two brothers from Shrewsbury.'

'Indeed!' said Adelais. 'What did they want with you?'

'The one of them was crippled, and went on crutches. He said he was once in your service, before he took the cowl. He remembered Father Wulfnoth. I thought they would have come to pay their respects to you. Did they not?'

She did not answer that, but only observed idly, gazing into distance as though only half her mind was on what was said: 'I remember, I did have a clerk once who entered the monastery at Shrewsbury. What was his business here at the church?'

'He said he had been spared by death, and was about making up all his accounts, to be better prepared. I found them beside the tomb of your lord's father. They were in some error that a woman of your house was buried there, eighteen years ago. The lame one had it in mind to spend a night's vigil there in prayers for her.'

'A strange mistake,' said Adelais with the same tolerant disinterest. 'No doubt you undeceived him?'

'I told him it was not so. I was not here then, of course, but I knew from Father Wulfnoth that the tomb had not been opened for many years, and what the young brother supposed could not be true. I told him that all of your house now are buried at Elford, where the head of the manor lies.'

'A long, hard journey that would be, for a lame man

afoot,' said Adelais with easy sympathy. 'I hope he did not intend to continue his travels so far?'

'I think, madam, he did. For they declined to rest and eat with me, and sleep the night over, but set off again at once. There I shall find her, the young one said. Yes, I am sure they will have turned eastward when they reached the high-road. A long, hard journey, indeed, but his will was good to perform it.'

His relationship with his patroness was a comfortable and easy one, he did not hesitate to ask directly: 'Will he indeed find the gentlewoman he's seeking at Elford?'

'He well may,' said Adelais, pacing evenly and serenely beside him. 'Eighteen years is a long time, and I cannot enter into his mind. I was younger then, I kept a bigger household. There were cousins, some left without fortune. My lord kept a father's hand on all of his blood. In his absence and as his regent, so did I.'

They had reached the churchyard gate, and halted there. The morning was soft and green, but very still, and the cloud-cover hung heavy and low.

'There will be more snow yet,' said the priest, 'if it does not turn to rain.' And he went on inconsequently: 'Eighteen years! It may be that this monk in his time with you was drawn to one of these young cousins, after the way of the young, and her early death was a greater grief to him than ever he ventured to let you know.'

'It may be so,' said Adelais distantly, and drew up the hood of her cloak against a few infinitely fine spears of sleet that drifted on the still air, and stung her cheek. 'Good day, Father!'

'I will pray,' said the priest after her, 'that his pilgrimage to her grave may bring comfort and benefit to him living, and to the lady dead.'

'Do so, Father,' said Adelais without turning her head. 'And do not fail to add a prayer for me and all the women of

63

my house, that time may lie lightly on us when our day comes.'

Caldfael lay awake in the hay-loft of a forester's holding in the royal forest of Chenet, listening to the measured breathing of his companion, too constant and too tense for sleep. it was the second night since they had left Hales. The first they had spent with a solitary cottar and his wife a mile or so beyond the hamlet of Weston, and the day between had been long, and this second shelter in the early reaches of the forest came very warmly and gratefully. They had gone early to their beds in the loft, for Haluin, at whose insistence they had continued so far into the evening, was close to exhaustion. Sleep, Cadfael noted, came to him readily and peacefully, a restoring mercy to a soul very troubled and wrung when awake. There are many ways by which God tempers the burden. Haluin rose every morning refreshed and resolute.

It was not yet light, there might still be an hour to dawn. There was no movement, no rustling of the dry hay from the corner where Haluin lay, but Cadfael knew he was awake now, and the stillness was good, for it meant that he lay in the languor of ease of body, wherever the wakeful mind within might have strayed.

'Cadfael?' said a still, remote voice out of the darkness, 'Are you awake?'

'I am,' he said as softly.

'You have never asked me anything. Of the thing I did. Of *her* . . .'

'There is no need,' said Cadfael. 'What you wish to tell will be told without asking.'

'I was never free to speak of her,' said Haluin, 'until now. And now only to you, who know.' There was a silence. He bled words slowly and arduously, as the shy and solitary do. After a while he resumed softly: 'She was not beautiful, as

64

her mother was. She had not that dark radiance, but something more kindly. There was nothing dark or secret in her, but everything open and sunlit, like a flower. She was not afraid of anything – not then. She trusted everyone. She had never been betrayed – not then. Only once, and she died of it.'

Another and longer silence, and this time the hay stirred briefly, like a sigh. Then he asked almost timidly: 'Cadfael, you were half your life in the world – did you ever love a woman?'

'Yes,' said Cadfael, 'I have loved.'

'Then you know how it was with us. For we did love, she and I. It hurts most of all,' said Brother Haluin, looking back in resigned and wondering pain, 'when you are young. There is nowhere to hide from it, no shield you can raise between. To see her every day . . . and to know that it was with her as it was with me . . .'

Even if he had put it from him all these years, and tried to turn hands and mind and spirit to the service he had undertaken, of his own will, in his extremity, he had forgotten nothing, it was there within him ready to quicken at a breath, like a sleeping fire when a door is opened. Now at least it could escape into air, into the world of other men, where it could touch other men's sufferings and receive and give compassion. From Cadfael there were no words needed, only the simple acknowledgement of companionship, the assurance of a listening ear.

Haluin fell asleep with a last lingering word on his lips, murmured almost inaudibly after lengthening silences. It might have been her name, Bertrade, or it might have been 'buried'. No matter! What mattered was that he had uttered it on the edge of sleep, and now would blessedly sleep again after all his harsh labour along the way, perhaps long past the coming of the light. So much the better! One day more spent on this pilgrimage might grieve his impatient spirit,

65

but it would certainly benefit his harshly driven body.

Cadfael arose very quietly, and left his companion deeply asleep and virtually a prisoner in the loft, since he would need help to get to his feet and descend the ladder. With the trapdoor left open, a listener below would hear when the sleeper stirred, but by the look of his relaxed body and the thin face smoothed of its tensions he would sleep for some time.

Cadfael went out into the clear, sharp morning, to snuff the still air, redolent of the lingering winter scents of forest-land still half asleep. From the forester's small assart among the trees it was possible to see the cleared grey of the track in broken glimpses between the old trunks, for the growth was close enough to keep the ground almost clear of under-brush. A handcart trundled along the road, laden with kindling from the fallen deadwood of the autumn, and the chattering flight of disturbed birds accompanied it in a shimmer of fluttered branches and drifting leaves. The forester was already up and about his morning tasks, his cow lumbering in to be milked, his dog weaving busily about his heels. A dry day, the sky overcast but lofty, the light good. A fine day for the road. By night they could be in Chenet itself, and the manor, in the king's holding, would take them in. Tomorrow to Lichfield, and there Cadfael was determined they should halt for another long night's rest, however ardently Haluin might argue for pressing on the remaining few miles to Elford. After a proper sleep in Lichfield Haluin should be in better condition to endure the next night's vigil pledged in Bertrade's memory, and face the beginning of the return journey, during which, God be praised, there need be no haste at all, and no cause to drive himself to the limits of endurance.

Sounds came muffled and soft along the beaten earth of the track, but Cadfael caught rather the vibration of hooves than the impact. Horses coming briskly from the west, two horses, for their gaits quivered in counterpoint, coming at a brisk trot, fresh from a night's rest and ready for the day. Travellers heading, perhaps, for Lichfield, after spending the night at the manor of Stretton, two miles back along the road. Cadfael stood to watch them pass.

Two men in dun-coloured gear, leather-coated, easy in the saddle, their seats and the handling of their mounts so strongly alike that either they had learned from childhood together, or the one had taught the other. And indeed, the one was double the bulk of the other and clearly a generation the elder, and though they were too distant and too briefly seen to have features, the whole shape of them indicated that they were kin. Two privileged grooms to some noble house, each with a woman pillion behind him. Women warmly cloaked for travelling look all much alike, and yet Cadfael stared after the first of these with roused attention, and kept his eyes on her until the horses and their riders had vanished along the road, and the soft drumming of hooves faded into distance.

She was still within his eyelids as he turned back into the hay-hut, pricking uneasily at his memory, urging, against all his dismissal of the possibility as folly, that he had seen her before, and further, that if he would but admit it he knew very well where.

But whether that was true or not, and whatever it augured if it was, there was nothing he could do about it. He shrugged it into the back of his mind, and went in, to listen for the moment when Haluin should awake and have need of him.

They came through groves of trees into an expanse of level meadows, a little bleached and grey as yet in the cold air, but fertile and well cultivated, a rich little island in a shire otherwise somewhat derelict still after the harsh pacification of fifty years back. There before them lay the sleek curves of the River Tame, the steep-pitched roof of a mill, and the close cluster of the houses of Elford, beyond the water.

In the warm and welcoming hospitality of the clerics of Lichfield they had spent a restful night, and received full directions as to the best road to Elford, and with the first light of dawn they had set off on the last four miles or so of this penitential journey. And here before them lay the goal of Haluin's pilgrimage, almost within reach, only an expanse of peaceful fields and a wooden footbridge between him and his absolution. A fortunate place, prosperous where much was impoverished, with not one mill by the waterside, but two, for they could see the second one upstream, with ample meadowland, and rich soil where the arable fields showed. A place that might well promise blessing and peace of mind after labour and pain.

The pale thread of the path led them forward, and the roofs of Elford rose before them, circled with trees and bushes still naked and dark at this distant view, not yet so far advanced in bud as to show the first faint, elusive smoke of green. They crossed the bridge, the uneven planks causing Haluin to watch carefully how he placed his crutches, and came into the track between the houses. A neat village, with housewives and husbandmen going cheerfully and confidently about their daily business, alert to strangers but civil and welcoming to the Benedictine habit. They exchanged greetings along the way, and Haluin, cheered and vindicated at the successful completion of his journey, began to flush and brighten with pleasure at being offered this spontaneous omen of acceptance and release.

No need to ask how to reach the church, they had seen its low tower before they crossed the bridge. It had been built since the Normans came, sturdy in grey stone, with a spacious churchyard very well stockaded for sanctuary at need, and full of old and handsome trees. They entered under the round-arched portico, and came into the familiar cool, echoing gloom of all stone-built churches, smelling faintly of dust, and wax candles, and strongly and reassuringly of home, the chosen abiding-place.

Haluin had halted in the tiled silence of the nave to get his bearings. Here there was no Lady Chapel to accommodate a patron's tomb between the altars, the lords of Elford must lie aside, built into the stones of the walls they had raised. The red eye of light from the altar lamp showed them where the tomb lay, a great table slab filling a niche in the right-hand wall. Some dead de Clary, perhaps the first who came over with King William, and got his reward later, showed as a sleeping figure in relief on the sealing stone. Haluin had started forward towards it, only to check and draw back after the first echoing step, for there was a woman on her knees beside the tomb.

They saw her only as a shadowy figure, for the cloak she wore was dark grey like the stone in this dim light, and they knew her for a woman and not a man because the hood of the cloak was thrown back from her head, uncovering a white linen coif and a gauze veil over it. They would have retired into the porch to let her complete her prayers in peace, but she had heard the impact of the crutches on the tiled floor, and turned her head sharply to look towards them. In a single graceful, abrupt movement she rose to her feet, and coming towards them, stepped into the light from a window, and showed them the proud, aging, beautiful face of Adelais de Clary.

Chapter Five

OU?' SHE said, staring, and turning her startled gaze from one face to the other, seeking, it seemed, some logic in this unexpected visitation. Her voice was neutral, neither welcoming nor repelling them. 'I had not thought to see you again so soon. Is there something more you have to ask of me, Haluin, that you have followed me here? You have only to ask. I have said I forgive.'

'Madam,' said Haluin, shaken and quivering from the apparition of his former mistress in this unexpected place, 'we have not followed you. Indeed I never thought to find you here. For your forbearance I'm grateful, and I would not for the world trouble you further. I have come here only in fulfilment of a vow I made. I had thought to spend a night in prayer at Hales, believing that my lady your daughter must be buried there. But we heard from the priest that it is not so. It's here at Elford she lies, in the tomb of her grandsires. So I have continued this far. And all I have to beg of you is your leave to keep my vigil here through this coming night, in deliverance of what I have sworn. Then we will depart, and trouble you no more.'

'I will not deny,' she said, but with a softening voice,

'that I shall be glad to have you gone. No ill-will! But this wound you have opened again for me I would willingly swathe away out of sight until it heals. Your face is a contagion that makes it open and bleed afresh. Do you think I should have taken horse and ridden here so fast if you had not put that old grief in my mind?'

'I trust,' said Haluin in a low and shaken voice, 'you may find, madam, as I hope to find, the wound cleansed of all its rancours by this atonement. It is my prayer that for you this time the healing may be sweet and wholesome.'

'And for you?' she said sharply, and turned a little away from him, with a motion of her hand that forbade any answer. 'Sweet and wholesome! You ask much of God, and more of me.' In the sidelong light from the window her face was fierce and sad. 'You have learned a monk's way with words,' she said. 'Well, it is a long time! Your voice was lighter once, so was your step. This at least I grant you, you are here at a very heavy cost. Do not deny me the grace of offering you rest and meat this time. I have a dwelling of my own here, within my son's manor pale. Come within and rest at least until Vespers, if you must punish your flesh on the stones here through the night.'

'Then I may have my night of prayer?' asked Haluin hungrily.

'Why not? Have you not just seen me entreating God in the same cause?' she said. 'I see you broken. I would not have you forsworn. Yes, have your penitential vigil, but take food in my house first. I'll send my grooms to fetch you,' she said, 'when you have made your devotions here.'

She was almost at the door, paying no attention to Haluin's hesitant thanks, and affording him no opportunity to refuse her hospitality, when she suddenly halted and swung round to them again.

'But say no word,' she said earnestly, 'to any other about your purpose here. My daughter's name and fame are safe

72

enough under the stone, let them lie quiet there. I would not have any other reminded as I have been reminded. Let it be only between us two, and this good brother who bears you company.'

'Madam,' said Haluin devoutly, 'there shall be no word said to any other soul but between us three, neither now nor at any other time, neither here nor in any other place.'

'You ease my mind,' she said, and in a moment she was gone, and the door drawn quietly to after her.

Haluin could not kneel without something firm before him to which to cling, and Cadfael's arm about him to ease his weight down gently, sharing the burden with his companion's one serviceable foot. They offered their dutiful prayer at the altar side by side, and Cadfael, open-eyed as Haluin kneeled long, traced with measured concern the worn lines of the young man's face. He had survived the hard journey afoot, but not without a heavy cost. The night on the stones here would be cold, cramping and long, but Haluin would insist on the last extreme of self-punishment. And after that, the long road back. As well, indeed, if the lady could persuade him to remain for at least a second night, if only as a concession and grace to her now they had, in a fashion, come to terms with their shared and haunted past.

For it could certainly be true that Haluin's sudden visit had sent her on her own pilgrimage, hotfoot here to confront her own part in that old tragedy. Passing by at a smart trot the forester's assart near Chenet, with only a maidservant and two grooms in her train, and striking an elusive spark in Cadfael's memory. It could well be true. Or would such a seed have borne fruit so fast? The implication of haste was there. Cadfael saw again the two double-laden horses passing in the early morning, going steadily and with purpose. In haste to pay a half-forgotten debt of affection and remorse? Or to arrive before someone else, and be ready and armed to receive him? She wanted them satisfied and gone, but that was natural enough. They had trespassed on her peace, and held up an old, flawed mirror before her beautiful face.

'Help me up!' said Haluin, and raised his arms like a child to be lifted to his feet; and that was the first time that he had asked for help, always before it had been proffered, and his acceptance humble and resigned rather than grateful.

'You did not speak one word throughout,' he said suddenly, marvelling, as they turned towards the church door.

'I had not one word to speak,' said Cadfael. 'But I heard many words. And even the silences between them were not altogether inarticulate.'

Adelais de Clary's groom was waiting for them in the porch, as she had promised, leaning indolently with one shoulder propped against the jamb of the door, as though he had been waiting for some time, but with immovable patience. His appearance confirmed everything Brother Cadfael had elaborated, in his own mind, from the few glimpses he had had of the riders between the trees. The younger of the pair, this, a brawny young man of perhaps thirty years, thickset, bull-necked, unmistakably in the Norman mould. Perhaps the third or fourth generation from a progenitor who had come over as a man-at-arms with the first de Clary. The strong original stock still prevailed, though intermarriage with English women had tempered the fairness of his hair into a straw-brown, and somewhat moderated the brutal bones of his face. He still wore his hair cropped into a close cap in the Norman manner, and his strong jaw clean-shaven, and he still had the bright, light, impenetrable eyes of the north. At their coming he sprang erect, more at ease in movement than in repose.

'My lady sends me to show you the way.'

His voice was flat and clipped, and he waited for no reply, but set off out of the churchyard before them, at a pace Haluin could not well maintain. The groom looked back at the gate and waited, and thereafter abated his speed, though it obviously chafed him to move slowly. He said nothing of his own volition, and replied to question or simple civility cordially enough, but briefly. Yes, Elford was a very fine property, good land and a good lord. Audemar's competent management of his honour was acknowledged indifferently; this young man's allegiance was to Adelais rather than to her son. Yes, his father was in the same service, and so had his father been before him. About these monastic guests he showed no curiosity at all, though he might have felt some. Those pale grey, alien eyes concealed all thought, or perhaps suggested thought's total absence.

He brought them by a grassy way to the gate of the manor enclosure, which was walled and spacious. Audemar de Clary's house sat squarely in the midst, the living floor raised well above a stone undercroft, and to judge by the small windows above there were at least two more chambers over the solar. And his ample courtyard was built round with other habitable rooms, as well as the customary and necessary stables, armoury, bakehouse and brewhouse, stores and workshops, and was populous with the activities of a large and busy household.

The groom led them to a small timber lodging under the curtain wall.

'My lady has had this chamber made ready for you. Use it as your own, she says, and the gateman will see to it you can come and go freely, to go to the church.'

Her hospitality, as they found, was meticulous but remote and impersonal. She had provided them with water for washing, comfortable pallets to rest on, sent them food from her own table, and given orders to tell them to ask for

75

anything they might need or want that had been forgotten, but she did not receive them into her own presence. Perhaps forgiveness did not reach so far as to render Haluin's remorseful presence agreeable to her. Nor was it her house-servants who waited on them, but the two grooms who had ridden with her from Hales. It was the elder of the two who brought them meat and bread and cheese, and small ale from the pantry. Cadfael had not been deceived in their relationship, for this one was clearly father to the other, a tough, square-set man in his fifties, close-mouthed like his son, broader in the shoulders, more bowed in the legs from years spent as much on horse-back as on his own two feet. The same cold, unconfiding eyes, the same bold and power-ful shaven jaws, but this one was tanned to a lasting bronze that Cadfael recognised from his own past as having its origin very far from England. His lord had been a crusader. This man had surely been with him there in the Holy Land, and got his burnished gloss there under the fierce, remem-bered sun.

The elder groom came again later in the afternoon, with a message not for Haluin but for Cadfael. It so happened that Haluin had fallen asleep on his pallet, and the man's entrance, light and soft as a cat for all his bulk, did not disturb his rest, for which Cadfael was grateful. There was a long and unrestful night to come. He motioned to the groom to wait, and went out into the courtyard to him, closing the door softly after him.

'Let him lie. He'll need to be wakeful later.'

'My lady told us how he means to spend the night,' said the groom. 'It's you she bids to her, if you'll come with me now. Let the other brother rest, she says, for he's been mortal sick. I grant him a man's guts, or he'd never have come so far on those feet. This way, Brother!'

Her dower dwelling was built into a corner of the curtain wall, sheltered from the prevailing winds, small, but

76

enough for such occasional visits as she chose to make to her son's court. A narrow hall and chamber, and a kitchen built lean-to against the wall outside. The groom strode in and through the hall with simple authority, as one having privilege here, and entered his mistress's presence much as a son or brother of hers might have done, trusting and trusted. Adelais de Clary was well served, but without subservience.

'Here is Brother Cadfael from Shrewsbury, my lady. The other one's asleep.'

Adelais was sitting at a distaff loaded with deep blue wool, spinning the spindle with her left hand, but at their entrance she ceased to turn it, and lodged it carefully against the foot of the distaff to prevent the yarn from uncoiling.

'Good! It's what he needs. Leave us now, Lothair, our guest will find his own way back. Is my son home yet?'

'Not yet. I'll be looking out for him when he comes.'

'He has Roscelin with him,' she said, 'and the hounds. When they're all home and kennelled and stalled, take your ease, it's well earned.'

He merely nodded by way of acknowledgement, and departed, taciturn and uneffusive as ever, and yet there was a tone in their exchanges of invulnerable assurance, secure as rooted rock. Adelais said no word until the door of her chamber had closed after her servant. She was eyeing Cadfael with silent attention, and the faint shadow of a smile.

'Yes,' she said, as if he had spoken. 'More than an old servant. He was with my lord all the years he fought in Palestine. More than once he did Bertrand that small service, to keep him man alive. It is another manner of allegiance, not a servant's. As bound in fealty as ever lord is to his overlord. I inherited what was my lord's before me. Lothair, he's called. His son is Luc. Born and bred in the same mould. You'll have seen the likeness, God knows it can hardly be missed.'

'I have seen it,' said Cadfael. 'And I knew where Lothair got that copper skin he wears.'

'Indeed?' She was studying him with concentrated interest now, having gone to the trouble to see him for the first time.

'I was some years in the east myself, before his time. If he lives long enough his brown will fade as mine has faded, but it takes a long while.'

'Ah! So you were not given to the monks in childhood. I thought you had not the look of such virgin innocents,' said Adelais.

'I entered of my own will,' said Cadfael, 'when it was time.'

'So did he – of his own will, though I think it was not time.' She stirred and sighed. 'I sent for you only to ask if you have everything you need – if my men have taken proper care of you.'

'Excellent care. And for their kindness and yours we are devoutly grateful.'

'And to ask you of him – of Haluin. I have seen in what sad case he is. Will it ever be better with him?'

'He will never walk as he did before,' said Cadfael, 'but as his sinews gain time and strength he will improve. He believed he was dying, so did we all, but he lives and will yet find much good in life – once his mind is at peace.'

'And will it be at peace after tonight? Is this what he needs?'

'I believe he will. I believe it is.'

'Then it has my blessing. And then you will take him back to Shrewsbury? I can provide you horses,' she said, 'for the way back. Lothair can fetch them to Hales when we return.'

'That kindness he will surely refuse,' said Cadfael. 'He has sworn to complete this penance on foot.'

She nodded understanding. 'I will ask him, none the less. Well – that is all, Brother. If he will not, I can do no more. Yes, one thing I can! I am coming to Vespers tonight, I will speak to the priest, and make certain that no one – no one! – shall question or trouble his vigil. You understand, nothing must be let slip to any soul but us who already know all too well. Tell him so. What remains is between him and God.'

The master of the house was just riding in at the gate as Cadfael walked back to the lodging where Haluin lay sleeping. The ring of harness and hooves and voices entered ahead of the cavalcade, a lively sound, bringing out grooms and servants like bees from a disturbed hive to attend on their lord's arrival. And here he came, Audemar de Clary on a tall chestnut horse, a big man in dark, plain, workmanlike riding clothes, without ornament, and needing none to mark him out as having authority here. He rode in with head uncovered, the hood of his short cloak flung back on his shoulders, and his shock of crisp hair was as dark as his mother's, but the powerful bones of his face, high-bridged nose, thrusting cheekbones and lofty forehead he surely had from his crusader father.

He could not, Cadfael thought, be yet forty years old. The vigour of his movements as he dismounted, the spring of his step on the ground, the very gestures of his hands as he stripped off his gloves, all were young. But the formidable features of his face and the mastery that was manifest all about him, in the efficiency of his management here and the prompt and competent service he expected and got, made him seem older in dominance than he was in years. He had been master, Cadfael recalled, in his father's long absence, beginning early, probably before he was twenty, and the de Clary honour was large and scattered. He had learned his business well. Not a man to be crossed lightly, but no one here feared him. They approached him cheerfully and spoke with him boldly. His anger, when justified, might be withering, even perilous, but it would be just.

He had a young fellow, page or squire, riding close at his elbow, a youth of seventeen or eighteen, fresh-faced and flushed with open air and exercise, and after them came two kennelmen on foot with the hounds on leash after their run. Audemar handed over his bridle to the groom who came running, and stood stamping his booted feet as he shed his cloak into the young man's ready hands. The brief flurry of activity was over in a few minutes, the horses on their way across the court to the stables, the hounds away to the kennels. The young groom Luc came out of the stable-yard and spoke to Audemar, apparently to deliver a message from Adelais, for Audemar at once looked round towards the lady's lodging, nodded understanding, and came striding towards her door. His eye fell on Cadfael, standing discreetly aside from his path, and for an instant he checked as though to stop and speak, but then changed his mind and went on, to vanish into the deep doorway.

Judging by the time that she and her grooms and her maid had passed by in the forest, Cadfael reckoned, Adelais must have arrived here that same day, two days previously. They would have no need to halt for a night between Chenet and Elford, on horseback the distance was easy. Therefore she must already have seen and talked with her son. What she had to communicate to him now, as soon as he returned from riding, might well have to do with whatever was news this day at the manor of Elford. And what was new but the arrival of the two monks from Shrewsbury, and their reason for being here, a reason she would interpret with discretion for him? For he had been here at Elford when his sister died in Hales, for the world's ears – and her brother's also? – of a fever. That must be all he had ever known of it, a simple, sad death, such as may happen in any household, even to one in the bloom of youth. No, that strong and resolute woman would never have let her son into the secret. An old, trusted, confidential maidservant, maybe. She must have needed such a one, now perhaps dead. But her young son, no, never.

And if that was true, no wonder Adelais was taking every precaution to smooth Haluin's way to his atonement, and be rid of him as quickly as possible, warding off all enquiry, even from the priest, offering horses to hasten the departure, and pledging the two pilgrims not to reveal anything of the past to any other being, not to say one word of the import of their errand, or mention the name of Bertrade.

Something, at least, I begin to understand, thought Cadfael. Wherever we turn, there is Adelais between us and all others. She houses us, she feeds us, it is her most loyal servants who approach and wait on us, not any from her son's household. My daughter's name and fame are safe enough under the stone, she had said, let them lie quiet there. Small blame to her for making sure, and no wonder she had ridden in haste to reach Elford beforehand and be ready for them.

And go we will, he thought, tomorrow morning if Haluin is fit to set out, and she can set her mind at rest. We can find another halting-place a mile or two from here, if we must, but at all costs we'll quit these walls, and she need never see or think of Haluin again.

The young squire had remained standing to watch his lord cross to the lady's door, Audemar's cloak flung over his shoulder, his bare head almost flaxen against the dark cloth. He had still the coltish, angular grace of youth. In a year or two his slenderness would fill out into solid and shapely manhood, with every movement under smooth control, but as yet he retained the vulnerable uncertainty of a boy. He looked after Audemar with surprised speculation, stared at Cadfael in candid curiosity, and turned slowly towards the door of Audemar's hall.

So this must be the Roscelin to whom Adelais had referred, thought Cadfael, watching him go. Not a son of the house, by the cut of him and the colouring, but not a servant, either. Doubtless a youngster from the family of one of Audemar's tenants, sent here to his overlord to get his training in arms, and acquire the skills and practices of a small court, in preparation for the wider world. Such apprentice lordlings proliferated in every great barony, the de Clary honour might well be patron to one or two of the same kind.

The early evening had turned cold, and there was a biting wind rising, with a few fine needles of sleet stinging in its touch. The hour of Vespers was not far away. Cadfael went in thankfully from the chill, to find Brother Haluin awake and waiting, silent and tense, for his hour of fulfilment.

Adelais had evidently made her dispositions well. No one intruded upon their privacy, no one asked any question or showed any curiosity. The young groom Luc brought them food before Vespers, and at the end of the office they were left alone in the church to conduct their vigil as they pleased. Doubtful if any among the household wondered about them at all, being accustomed to random visitors of all kinds, with differing needs, and the devotions of a pair of itinerant Benedictines surprised no one. If monks of the abbey of Saint Peter elected to spend a night in prayer in a church of Saint Peter, that was no special wonder, and concerned no one else.

So Brother Haluin had his will, and redeemed his vow. He would have no softening of the stone, no extra cloak to ward off the cold of the night, nothing to abate the rigours of his penance. Cadfael helped him to his knees, within reach of the solid support of the tomb, so that if faintness or dizziness came over him he could at least hold fast by it to break his fall. The crutches were laid at the foot of the stone. There was no more he would permit anyone to do for him. But Cadfael kneeled with him, withdrawn into shadow to leave him solitary with his dead Bertrade and a God doubtless inclining a compassionate ear.

It was a long night, and cold. The altar lamp made an eye of brightness in the gloom, at least ruddy like fire if it gave no warmth. The silence carried hour by hour, like an infinitesimal ripple vibrating through it, the gradual heave of Haluin's breathing and the constant whisper of his moving lips, felt in the blood and the bowels rather than audible with the ear. From somewhere within him he drew an inexhaustible wealth of words to be spent for his dead Bertrade. Their tension and passion kept him erect and oblivious to pain, though pain took fast hold of him before midnight, and never left him until his rapture and his ordeal ended together with the coming of the light.

When he opened his eyes at last to the full light of a frosty morning, and laboriously unlocked his cold, clasped hands, the sounds of the customary early activity were already audible from the outside world. Haluin stared dazedly upon the waking day, returning from some place very far off, very deep within. He essayed to move, to grip the rim of the stone, and his fingers were so numbed they could not feel, and his arms so stiff they could give him no help to raise himself. Cadfael wound an arm about him to lift him, but Haluin could not straighten his stiff knees to set his better foot to the ground, but hung a dead weight on the encircling arm. And suddenly there was a flurry of light footsteps, and another arm, young and strong, embraced the helpless body from the other side, a fair head stooped to Haluin's shoulder, and between his two supporters he was hauled upright, and held so as the blood flowed back achingly into his numbed legs.

'In God's name, man,' said the young man Roscelin

impatiently, 'must you use yourself so hardly when you have already enough for any sane man to carry?'

Haluin was too startled, and his mind still too far away, to be capable of grasping that, much less answering it. And if Cadfael privately considered it a perfectly sensible reaction, aloud he said practically: 'Keep firm hold of him, so, while I pick up his crutches. And God bless you for appearing so aptly. Spare to scold him, you'd be wasting your breath. He's under vow.'

'A foolish vow!' said the boy with the arrogant certainty of his years. 'Who's the better for this?' But for all his disapproval he held Haluin warmly and firmly, and looked at him sidelong with a frown at least as anxious as it was exasperated.

'He is,' said Cadfael, propping the crutches under Haluin's armpits, and setting to work to chafe life back into the cold hands that could not yet grip the staves. 'Hard to believe, but you had better credit it. There, you can let him lean on his props now, but hold him steady. Well for you at your years, you can sleep easy, with nothing to regret and nothing to ask pardon for. How did you come to look in here so timely?' he asked, eyeing the young man with fresh interest, thus at close quarters. 'Were you sent?'

For this boy seemed an unlikely instrument for Adelais to use in shepherding her inconvenient guests in and out of Elford – too young, too blunt, too innocent.

'No,' said Roscelin shortly, and relented to add with better grace: 'I was plain curious.'

'Well, that's human,' admitted Cadfael, recognising his own besetting sin.

'And this morning Audemar has no immediate work for me, he's busy with his steward. Had we not better get this brother of yours back to his lodging, where it's warmer? How shall we do? I can fetch a horse for him if we can get him mounted.'

84

Haluin had come back from his distant place to find himself being discussed and handled as if he had no mind of his own, and no awareness of his surroundings. He stiffened instinctively against the indignity. 'No,' he said, 'I thank you, but I can go now. I need not trespass on your kindness further.' And he flexed his hands and gripped the staves of his crutches, and took the first cautious steps away from the tomb.

They followed closely, one at either elbow in case he faltered, Roscelin going before up the shallow steps and through the doorway to prevent a possible stumble, Cadfael coming close behind to support him if he reeled backwards. But Haluin had gathered to his aid a will refreshed and strengthened by achievement, and was resolute to manage this walk alone, at whatever cost. And there was no haste. When he felt the need he could rest on his crutches to draw breath, and so he did three times before they reached Audemar's courtyard, already populous and busy about bakery and mews and well-head. It said much for young Roscelin's quickness and delicacy of mind, Cadfael reflected, that he waited without comment or impatience at every pause, and refrained from offering a hand in help until help should be invited. So Haluin came back to the lodging in Audemar's courtyard as he would have wished, on his own misshapen feet, and could feel that he had earned the ease of his bed.

Roscelin followed them in, still curious, in no haste to go in search of whatever duties awaited him. 'Is that all, then?' he said, watching Haluin stretch out his still numbed limbs gratefully, and draw the brychan over them. 'Then where do you go when you leave us? And when? You'll not set out today?'

'We go back to Shrewsbury,' said Cadfael. 'Today – that I doubt. A day's rest would be wisdom.' By the weary ease of Haluin's face, and the softened gaze turned inward, it would not be long before he fell asleep, the best and best-earned sleep since he had made his confession.

'I saw you ride in with the lord Audemar yesterday,' said Cadfael, studying the youthful face before him. 'The lady mentioned your name. Are you kin to the de Clarys?'

The boy shook his head. 'No. My father is tenant and vassal to him, they've always been good friends, and there's a marriage tie, a while back now. No, I'm sent here to Audemar's service at my father's order.'

'But not at your wish,' said Cadfael, interpreting the tone rather than the words.

'No! Much against my wish!' said Roscelin abruptly, and scowled at the floorboards between his booted feet.

'Yet to all appearances as good a lord as you could hope for,' suggested Cadfael mildly, 'and better than most.'

'He's well enough,' the boy owned fairly. 'I've no complaint of *him*. But I grudge it that my father has sent me away here to be rid of me out of the house, and that's the truth of it.'

'Now why,' wondered Cadfael, curious but not quite asking, 'why should any father want to be rid of you?' For here was undoubtedly the very picture of a presentable son, upstanding, well-formed, well-conducted, and decidedly engaging in his fair-haired, smooth-cheeked comeliness, a son any father would be glad to parade before his peers. Even in sullenness his face was pleasing, but it was certainly true that he had not the look of one happy in his service.

'He has his reasons,' said Roscelin moodily. 'You'd say good reasons, too, I know that. And I'm not so estranged from him that I could refuse him the obedience due. So I'm here, and pledged to stay here unless lord and father both give me leave to go. And I'm not such a fool as not to admit I could be in far worse places. So I may as well get all the good I can out of it while I'm here.'

It seemed that his mind had veered into another and graver quarter, for he sat for some moments silent, staring down into his clasped hands with a frowning brow, and looked up only to measure Cadfael earnestly, his eyes dwelling long upon the black habit and the tonsure.

'Brother,' he said abruptly, 'I've wondered, now and then – about the monkish life. Some men have taken to it, have they not, because what they most wanted was for ever impossible – forbidden them! Is that true? Can it provide a life, if . . . if the life a man wants is out of reach?'

'Yes,' said Brother Haluin's voice, gently and quietly out of a waking dream now very close to sleep. 'Yes, it can!'

'I would not recommend entering it as a second-best,' said Cadfael stoutly. Yet that was what Haluin had done, long ago, and he spoke now as one recording a revelation, the opening of his inward eyes just as they were heavy and closing with sleep.

'The time might be long, and the cost high,' said Haluin with gentle certainty, 'but in the end it would not be second-best.'

He drew in a long breath, and spent it in a great healing sigh, turning his head away from them on the pillow. They were both so intent on him, doubting and wondering, that neither of them had noted the approach of brisk footsteps without, and they started round in surprise as the door was thrown wide open to admit Lothair, carrying a basket of food and a pitcher of small ale for the guests. At the sight of Roscelin seated familiarly upon Cadfael's pallet, and apparently on good terms with the brothers, the groom's weathered face tightened perceptibly, almost ominously, and for an instant a deeper spark flashed and vanished again in his pale eyes.

'What are you doing here?' he demanded with the bluntness of an equal, and the uncompromising authority of an elder. 'Master Roger's looking for you, and my lord wants you in attendance as soon as he's broken his fast. You'd best be off, and sharp about it, too.'

It could not be said that Roscelin showed any alarm at this intelligence, or resentment at the manner in which it was delivered, rather the man's assurance seemed to afford him a little tolerant amusement. But he rose at once, and with a nod and a word by way of farewell went off obediently but without haste to his duty. Lothair stood narrow-eyed in the doorway to watch him go, and did not come fully into the room with his burdens until the boy had reached the steps to the hall door.

Our guard-dog, thought Cadfael, has his orders to ward off any others who come too close, but he had not reckoned with having to do as much for young Roscelin. Now could there, I wonder, be some reason why that contact in particular should cause him consternation? For that's the first spark I've seen struck from his steel!

Chapter Six

DELAIS herself paid a gracious visit to her monastic guests after Mass, with solicitous enquiries after their health and wellbeing. It was possible, Cadfael reflected, that Lothair had reported back to her the inconvenient and undesirable incursion of the young man Roscelin into a preserve she clearly wished to keep private. She appeared in the doorway of their small chamber, prayer-book in hand, alone, having sent her maid on ahead to her dower house. Haluin was awake, and made to rise from his pallet in respectful acknowledgement of her coming, reaching in haste for his crutches, but she motioned him back with a wave of her hand.

'No, be still! No ceremony is needed between us. How do you find yourself now – now that your vow is accomplished? I hope you have experienced grace, and can return to your cloister in peace. I wish you that mercy. An easy journey and a safe arrival!'

And above all, thought Cadfael, an early departure. And small blame to her. It's what I want, too, and so must Haluin. To have this matter finished, neatly and cleanly, with no more harm to any creature, with mutual forgiveness, once spoken, and thereafter silence.

'You have had little rest,' she said, 'and have a long journey back to Shrewsbury. My kitchen shall supply you with food for the first stages of the way. But I think you should also accept horses. I have said so to Brother Cadfael already. The stables here can spare you mounts, and I will send for them to Hales when I return there. You should not attempt to go back all that way on foot.'

'For the offer, and for all your kindness, we are grateful,' said Haluin in instant and hasty protest. 'But this I cannot accept. I undertook both to go and to return on foot, and I must make good what I vowed. It is a pledge of faith that I am not so crippled as to be utterly useless and unprofitable hereafter, to God and man. You would not wish me to go home shamed and forsworn.'

She shook her head over his obstinacy with apparent resignation. 'So your fellow here warned me you would argue, when I spoke of it to him, but I hoped you would see better reason. Surely you are also pledged to return to your duty at the abbey as soon as may be. Has that no force? If you insist on going afoot you cannot set out at least until tomorrow, after so hard a night on the stones.'

To Haluin, no doubt, that sounded like true solicitude, and an invitation to delay until he was fully rested. To Cadfael it had the sound of a subtle dismissal.

'I never thought that it would be easy,' said Haluin, 'to perform what I swore. Nor should it be. The whole virtue, if there is any virtue in it at all, is to endure the hardship and complete the penance. And so I can and shall. You are right, I owe it to my abbot and my brothers to get back to my duty as soon as I may. We must set out today. There are still hours of daylight left, we must not waste them.'

To do her justice, she did seem to be taken aback at such ready compliance with what she wished, even if she had not expressed the wish. She urged, though without warmth, the necessity of rest, but gave way pliantly before Haluin's stubborn insistence. Things had gone as she wished, at the last moment she could afford one brief convulsion of pity and regret.

'It must be as you wish,' she said. 'Very well, Luc shall bring you food and drink before you go, and fill your scrip for you. As for me, I part from you in goodwill. Now and hereafter, I wish you well.'

When she was gone, Haluin sat silent for a while, shivering a little in the recoil from the finality of this ending. It was as he had hoped, and yet it left him shaken.

'I have made things needlessly hard for you,' he said ruefully. 'You must be as weary as I am, and I have committed you to leaving thus, without sleep. She wanted us gone, and for my part I heartily wish to be gone. The sooner severed, the better for us all.'

'You did right,' said Cadfael. 'Once out of here we need not go far, you are in no case to attempt it today. But to be out of here is all we need.'

They left Audemar de Clary's manor gates in mid-afternoon, under a sky heavy with grey cloud, and turned westward along the track through Elford village, with a chill, insidious wind in their faces. It was over. From this point on, with every step taken they were returning to normality and safety, to the monastic hours and the blessed daily round of work, worship and prayer.

From the highroad Cadfael looked back once, and saw the two grooms standing in the gateway to watch the guests depart. Two solid, sturdy figures, taciturn and inscrutable, following the withdrawal of the interlopers with light, fierce northern eyes. Making sure, thought Cadfael, that the disquiet we brought to that lady departs with us, and leaves no shadow behind.

They did not look back a second time. The need now was to put at least one safe, alienating mile between themselves

91

and the dower house of Elford, and after that they could look for a night's shelter early, for in spite of his resolution it was clear that Haluin was haggard and grey with exhaustion, and would not get far without danger of collapse. His face was set to endure, he went steadily but heavily on his crutches, his eyes dilated and dark in their deep hollows. Doubtful if even now he enjoyed the peace he should have found at Bertrade's tomb, but perhaps it was not Bertrade who still haunted his thoughts.

'I shall never see her again,' said Haluin, to God, himself and the gathering dusk rather than to Cadfael. And it was hard to say whether he spoke in relief or regret, as at leaving something unfinished.

The first snow of a capricious March burst upon them suddenly out of the lowering sky when they were some two miles from Elford. The air was on the edge of frost, there would be no great or prolonged fall, but while it lasted it was thick and blinding, stinging their faces and confusing the path before them. The premature dusk closed down on them almost abruptly, a murky darkness out of which whirling clouds of white flakes wound about them bewilderingly, veiling even what landmarks they had on a stretch of track open, windswept and treeless.

Haluin had begun to stumble, troubled by the driven flakes filling his eyes, and unable to free a hand to draw the folds of his cowl together against the assault. Twice he planted a crutch aside from the trodden path, and all but fell. Cadfael halted and stood close, his back to the wind, to give his companion breathing space and shelter for some moments, while he considered where they were, and what he could recall of the surrounding country from their outward journey. Any dwelling, however mean, would be welcome until this squall blew over. Somewhere here, he calculated, there had been a side-path bearing north, and leading to what seemed to be a cluster of small houses and the long pale of a manor fence, the only sign of occupation within view of the road.

His recollection was accurate. Going cautiously before, with Haluin close at his back, he came to an isolated clump of bushes and low trees which he remembered clearly in this sparsely treed plain, and a little beyond these the path opened. There was even a flickering spark of torchlight, seen fitfully through the whirling snowfall, to keep them in the direct way towards the distant dwelling. Where the lord of the house showed a beacon for benighted travellers there should be a warm welcome waiting.

It took them longer to reach the hamlet than Cadfael had expected, since Haluin was flagging badly, and it was necessary to go very slowly, reaching back constantly to keep him close. Here and there a solitary tree loomed suddenly out of the spinning whiteness on the left hand or the right, only to be veiled again as abruptly. The flakes had grown larger and wetter, the hint of frost was receding, and this fall would not lie beyond the morning. Overhead the clouds were broken and torn in a rising wind, with a scattering of stars showing through.

The spark of torchlight had vanished, hidden behind the manor fence. A solid timber gatepost heaved out of the dark, the tall palisade running away from it on the left hand, the broad open gateway on the right, and suddenly there was the torch again, across a wide courtyard in a sconce jutting from under the eaves, to light the stair that climbed to the hall door. The usual encrustation of service buildings lined the stockade. Cadfael launched a shout ahead of their lurching entrance, and a man came butting his way through the falling snow from a stable door, shouting to others as he came. At the head of the steps the hall door opened on a welcome glimpse of firelight.

Cadfael brought Haluin stumbling in through the open

gate in his arm, and another willing arm took him about the body on the other side, hoisting him vigorously into the comparative shelter within the pale. A voice bellowed heartily through the snowfall: 'Brothers, you chose a bad night to be out on the roads. Hold up, now, your troubles are over. We never shut the gates on your cloth.'

There were others coming forth by then to bring in the benighted travellers, a young fellow darting out from the undercroft with a sacking hood over head and shoulders, a bearded and gowned elder emerging from the hall and coming halfway down the steps to meet them. Haluin was lifted rather than led up the steep flight and into the hall, where the master of the house came striding out of his solar to meet these unexpected arrivals.

A fair man, long-boned and sparsely fleshed, with a short trimmed beard the colour of wheat straw, and a thick cap of hair of the same shade. Perhaps in his late thirties, Cadfael thought, of a ruddy, open countenance in which the blue Saxon eyes shone almost startlingly bright, candid and concerned.

'Come in, come in, Brothers! Well that you've found us! Here, bring him through here, close to the fire.' He had taken in at once the Benedictine habits, the flurries of snow lodged in the folds, and shaken off now hissing into the steady fire in the central hearth of the hall, the crippled feet of his younger visitor, the drawn grey exhaustion of his face. 'Edgytha, have beds prepared in the end chamber, and tell Edwin to mull more wine.'

His voice was loud, solicitous and warm. Without seeming haste he had his servants running here and there on his benevolent errands, and himself saw Haluin installed on a bench against the wall, where the warmth of the fire could reach him.

'This young brother of yours is in very sad case,' said the host, aside to Cadfael, 'to be travelling the roads so far from home. There are none of your order round here – barring the sisters at Farewell, the bishop's new foundation. From which house do you come?'

'From Shrewsbury,' said Cadfael, setting Haluin's crutches to lean against the bench, where he could reach them at will. Haluin sat back with closed eyes, his grey cheeks slowly gaining a little colour in the warmth and ease.

'So far? Could not your abbot have sent a hale man on his errands, if he had business in another shire?'

'This was Haluin's own errand,' said Cadfael. 'No other could have done it. Now it's done, and we're on our way home, and by stages we shall get there. Always with the help of hospitable souls like you. Can I ask, what is this place? These are parts I hardly know.'

'My name is Cenred Vivers. From this manor I take that name. This brother is called Haluin, you say? And yourself?'

'Cadfael is my name. Born Welsh, and bred up on the borders with a foot either side. I've been a brother of Shrewsbury now more than twenty years. My business on this journey is simply to keep Haluin company and see that he gets safely to where he's going, and safely back again.'

'No easy matter,' agreed Cenred, low-voiced, and eyeing Haluin's deformed feet ruefully, 'the state he's in. But if the work's done and only the way home to venture, no doubt you'll do it. How did he come by such injuries?'

'He fell from a roof. We had repairs to do, in the hard weather before Christmas. It was the slates falling after him that cut his feet to ribbons. Well that we kept him alive.'

They were speaking of him softly, a little aside, though he lay back as eased and still as if he had fallen asleep, his eyes closed, the long dark lashes shadowing his hollow cheeks. The hall had emptied about them, all the bustle of activity withdrawn elsewhere, busy with pillows and brychans and the hospitable business of the kitchen.

'They're slow with the wine,' said Cenred, 'and you must both need some warmth inside you. If you'll hold me excused, Brother, I'll go and hasten things in the pantry.'

And he was off, the flurry and wind of his passing causing Haluin's closed eyelids to quiver. In a moment he opened his eyes and looked slowly and dazedly about him, taking in the warm, high-roofed dimness of the hall, the glow of the fire, the heavy hangings that screened two alcoves withdrawn from the public domain, and the half-open door of the solar from which Cenred had emerged. The pale, steady gleam of candle-light showed from within.

'Have I dreamed?' wondered Haluin, gazing. 'How did we come here? What place is this?'

'Never fear,' said Cadfael, 'on your own two feet you came here, only an arm to help you up the steps into the house. The manor is called Vivers, and the lord of it is Cenred. We've fallen into good hands.'

Haluin drew deep breath. 'I am not so strong as I believed I was,' he said sadly.

'No matter, you can rest now. We have left Elford behind.'

They were both speaking in low voices, a little awed by the enfolding silence presiding even in the centre of this populous household. When both ceased speaking, the quietness seemed almost expectant. And in the hush the half-open door of the solar opened fully upon the pale gold candle-light within, and a woman stepped into the doorway. For that one instant she was sharply outlined as a shadow against the soft light within, a slender, erect figure, mature and dignified in movement, surely the lady of the house and Cenred's wife. The next moment she had taken two or three light, swift steps into the hall, and the light of the nearest torch fell upon her shadowy face and advancing form, and conjured out of the dim shape a very different person. Everything about her was changed. Not a gracious

96

chatelaine of more than thirty years, but a rounded, fresh-faced girl, no more than seventeen or eighteen, half her oval countenance two great startled eyes and the wide, high fore-head above them, white and smooth as pearl.

Haluin uttered a strange, soft sound in his throat, between gasp and sigh, clutched at his crutches and heaved himself to his feet, staring at this sudden glowing apparition as she, brought up abruptly against the intrusion of strangers, had drawn back in haste, staring at him. For one moment they hung so, mute and still, then the girl whirled about and retreated into the solar, drawing the door to almost stealthily after her.

Haluin's hands slackened their hold, dangling inertly, the crutches slid and fell from under him, and he went down on his face in a gradual, crumpled fall, and lay senseless in the rushes of the floor.

They carried him to a bed prepared for him in a quiet chamber withdrawn from the hall, and bedded him there, still in a deep swoon.

'This is simple exhaustion,' said Cadfael in reassurance to Cenred's solicitous anxiety. 'I knew he was driving him-self too hard, but that's done with now. From this on we can take our time. Leave him to sleep through this night, and he'll do well enough. See, he's coming round. His eyes are opening.'

Haluin stirred, his eyelids quivering before they rose on the dark, sharply conscious eyes within, that looked up into a circle of vague, concerned faces. He was aware of his surroundings, and knew what had happened to him before he was carried here, for the first words he spoke were in meek apology for troubling them, and thanks for their care.

'My fault!' he said. 'It was presumptuous to attempt too much. But now all is well with me. All is very well!'

97

Since his chief need was clearly of rest, they were left to make themselves comfortable in their small chamber, though the evening brought them a number of visits. The bearded steward brought them hot, spiced wine, and sent in to them the old woman Edgytha, who brought them water for their hands, food, and a lamp, and offered whatever more they might need for their comfort.

She was a tall, wiry, active woman probably sixty years old, with the free manner and air of authority habitual in servants who have spent many years in the confidence of lord or lady, and earned a degree of trust that brings with it acknowledged privilege. The younger maidservants deferred to her, if they did not actually go in awe of her, and her neat black gown and stiff white wimple, and the keys jingling at her waist bore witness to her status.

Late in the evening she came again, in attendance on a plump and pleasant lady, soft-voiced and gracious, who came to enquire kindly whether the reverend brothers had all that they needed for the night, and whether the one who had swooned was now comfortably recovered from his faintness. Cenred's wife was rosily pretty, brown-haired and brown-eyed, a very different creature from the tall, slender, vulnerable young thing who had stepped out of the solar, to be startled into recoil from the unexpected apparition of strangers.

'And have the lord Cenred and his lady any children?' Cadfael asked when their hostess was gone.

Edgytha was close-lipped, possessively protective of her family and all that was theirs, to the point of rendering every such enquiry suspect, but after a moment's hesitation she answered civilly enough: 'They have a son, a grown son.' And she added, unexpectedly reconsidering her reluctance to satisfy such uncalled-for curiosity: 'He's away, in service with my lord Cenred's overlord.'

There was a curious undertone of reserve, even of

disapproval, in her voice, though she would never have acknowledged it. It almost distracted Cadfael's mind from his own preoccupation, but he pursued delicately:

'And no daughter? There was a young girl looked into the hall for a moment, while we were waiting. Is she not a child of the house?'

She gave him a long, steady, searching look, with raised brows and tight lips, plainly disapproving of such interest in young women, coming from a monastic. But guests in the house must be treated with unfailing courtesy, even when they fall short of deserving it.

'That lady is the lord Cenred's sister,' she said. 'The old lord Edric, his father, married a second time in his later years. More like a daughter to him than a sister, with the difference in years. I doubt you'll see her again. She would not wish to disturb the retirement of men of your habit. She has been well brought up,' concluded Edgytha with evident personal pride in the product of her own devotion, and a plain warning that black monks cast by chance into the household should keep their eyes lowered in a young virgin's presence.

'If you had her in charge,' said Cadfael amiably, 'I make no doubt she does credit to her upbringing. Had you Cenred's boy in your care, too?'

'My lady would not have dreamed of trusting her chick to any other.' The old woman had warmed into fond fervour in thinking of the children she had nursed. 'No one ever had the care of better babes,' she said, 'and I love them both like my own.'

When she was gone Haluin lay silent for a while, but his eyes were open and clear, and the lines of his face alert and aware.

'Was there indeed a girl who came in?' he said at last, frowning in the effort to recall a moment which had become hazy and uncertain in his mind. 'I have been lying here trying to recall why I so started up. I remember the crutches dropping away from under me, but very little besides. Coming into the warmth made my head go round.'

'Yes,' said Cadfael, 'there was a girl. Half-sister, it seems, to Cenred, but younger by some twenty years. If you were thinking you dreamed her, no, she was no dream. She came into the hall from the solar, all unaware of us, and perhaps not liking the look of us, she drew back again in haste and closed the door between. Do you not remember that?'

No, he did not remember it, or only as an unconnected snatch of vision comes back out of a dream, and is gone again as soon as glimpsed. He frowned after it anxiously, and shook his head as if to clear eyes misted by weariness. 'No . . . there's nothing clear to me. I do recall the door opening, I take your word for it she came in . . . but I can recall nothing, no face . . . Tomorrow, perhaps.'

'We shall see no more of her,' said Cadfael, 'if that devoted dragon of hers has any say in the matter. I think she has no very high opinion of monks, Mistress Edgytha. Well, are you minded for sleep? Shall I put out the lamp?'

But if Haluin had no clear recollection of the daughter of the house, no image left from that brief glimpse of her, first a dark outline against candle-light, then lit from before by the ruddy glow of the torch, Cadfael had a very clear image, one that grew even clearer when the lamp was quenched and he lay in the dark beside his sleeping companion. And beyond the remembrance he had a strange, disquieting sense that it bore for him a special significance, if he could but put his finger on it. Why that should be so was a mystery to him. Wakeful in the dark, he called up the features of her face, the motion of her body as she stepped into the light, and could find nothing there that should have been meaningful to him, no likeness to any woman he had ever seen before, except as all women are sisters. Yet the sense of some elusive familiarity about her persisted.

A tall girl, though perhaps not so tall as she gave the impression of being, for her slenderness contributed to the image, but above the middle height for a girl just becoming woman. Her bearing was erect and graceful, but still with the tentative and vulnerable springiness of the child, the suddenness of a lamb or a fawn, alert to every sound and motion. Startled, she had sprung back from them, and yet she had closed the door with measured softness, not to startle in return. And her face – she was not beautiful, except as youth and innocence and gallantry are always beautiful. An oval face she had, tapered from broad brow and wide and wide-set eyes to the firm, rounded chin. Her head was uncovered, her brown hair drawn back and braided, still further emphasising the high white brow and the great eyes under their level dark brows and long lashes. The eyes consumed half the face. Not pure brown, Cadfael thought, for in spite of their darkness they had a clarity and depth and brightness perceptible even in that one glimpse of her. Rather a dark hazel shot with green, and so clear and deep it seemed possible to plunge into them and drown. Eyes utterly candid and vulnerable, and quite fearless. Young, wild, mettlesome creatures of the woods, never yet hunted or harmed, may have that look. And the pure, fine lines of her cheekbones Cadfael remembered, elegant and strong, after the eyes her chief distinction.

And in all of this, sharply defined in his mind's eye, what was there to trouble him, to pierce him like an elusive memory of some other woman? He found himself summoning up, one by one, the faces of women he had known, half the population of a long and varied life, in case some cast of features or carriage of head or gesture of hand should strike the chord that would vibrate and sing for him. But there was no match, and no echo. Cenred's sister remained unique and apart, haunting him thus only because she had appeared and vanished in a moment, and he would probably never see her again.

Nevertheless, the last fleeting vision within his eyelids as he fell asleep was of her startled face.

By morning the air had lost its frosty bite, and most of the snow that had fallen had already thawed and vanished, leaving its tattered laces along the foot of every wall and under the bole of every tree. Cadfael looked out from the hall door, and was inclined to wish that the fall had persisted, to prevent Haluin from insisting on taking to the road again immediately. As it turned out he need not have worried, for as soon as the manor was up and about its daily business Cenred's steward came looking for them, with the request that they would come to his lord in the solar after they had broken their fast, for he had something to ask of them.

Cenred was alone in the room when they entered, Haluin's crutches sounding hollowly on the boards of the floor. The room was lit by two deep, narrow windows with cushioned seats built into them, and furnished with handsome bench-chests along one wall, a carved table, and one princely chair for the lord's use. Evidently the lady Emma ran a well-regulated household, for hangings and cushions were of fine embroidery, and the tapestry frame in one corner, with its half-finished web of bright colours, showed that they were of home production.

'I hope you have slept well, Brothers,' said Cenred, rising to greet them. 'Are you recovered fully from last night's indisposition? If there is anything my house has failed to offer you, you have but to ask for it. Use my manor as you would your own dwelling. And you will, I hope, consent to stay yet a day or two before you need set out again.'

Cadfael shared the hope, but was all too afraid that

Haluin would rouse his over-anxious conscience to find objections. But he had no time to do more than open his mouth, for Cenred went on at once:

'For I have something to ask of you . . . Is either of you ordained a priest?'

Chapter Seven

ES,' SAID Haluin, after a moment of blank silence. 'I am a priest. I studied for minor orders from the time I entered the abbey, and became full priest when I reached thirty years. We are encouraged to do so now, those who enter young and are already lettered. As a priest, what is there I can do to serve you?'

'I want you to conduct a marriage,' said Cenred.

This time the silence was longer, and their concentration on him more wary and thoughtful. For if a marriage was contemplated in this house, surely provision would already have been made for a priest, and one who knew the circumstances and the parties, not a chance Benedictine benighted here by a fall of snow. Cenred saw their doubts reflected in Haluin's attentive face.

'I know what you would say. This must surely be the proper business of my own parish priest. There is no church here in Vivers, though I intend to build and endow one. And it so happens that our nearest parish church is at this moment without a priest until it pleases the bishop to name his choice, for the advowson is with him. I had meant to send for a cousin of our house who is in orders, but if you are willing we may spare him a wintry journey. I promise you there is nothing underhand in this matter, and if it is being arranged in some haste, there are sound reasons. Sit down with me, at least, and I'll tell you freely all you need to know, and you shall judge.'

With the impulsive and generous vehemence that seemed to be natural to him, he strode forward himself to support Haluin by the forearms as he lowered himself to the cushioned bench built against the panelled wall. Cadfael sat down beside his friend, content to watch and listen, since he was no priest, and here had no hard decision to consider, and the delay came gratefully to him for Haluin's sake.

'In his old age,' said Cenred, coming bluntly to the business in hand, 'my father married a second time, a wife thirty years younger than he was. I was already married, with a son a year old, when my sister Helisende was born. Those two children grew up in this house, boy and girl together, like brother and sister, and close at that. And we, their elders, have taken them for granted and been glad they should have each other's company. I have been much to blame. I never noticed when they began to be more than playmates. I never thought how childish companionship and affection could change so after years, into something more perilous by far. I do not blink away facts, Brothers, once I have seen them, and been forced to see them. Those two were left alone to play too long and too lovingly. They have slipped into an inordinate affection under my very nose, and I stone blind to it until almost too late. They love each other in a fashion and to a degree that is anathema between two so closely kin. Thanks be to God, they have not sinned in the flesh, not yet. I hope I have awakened in time. God knows I want what is best for them both, I would have them happy, but what happiness can there be in a love which is an abomination? Better by far to tear them apart now, and trust to time to take away the pain. I have sent my son to serve his apprenticeship to arms with my overlord, who is a good friend, and knows the reason and the need. And sore as he is at being banished so, my son has pledged himself not to return until I give him leave. Have I done right?'

'I think,' said Haluin slowly, 'you could have done no other. But it is a pity it went so far unchecked.'

'So it is. But when two grow up from babes together as brother and sister, that in itself is commonly enough to put away from them without grief all thought of affection after the way of marriage. I have wondered sometimes how much Edgytha noticed that I did not. She indulged them always. But never, never did she say word to me or my wife, and whether I have done well or not, I must go on.'

'Tell me,' said Cadfael, speaking for the first time, 'is not your son's name Roscelin?'

Cenred's eyes flashed to Cadfael's face, astonished. 'So it is, But how can you know that?'

'And your overlord is Audemar de Clary. Sir, we came hither directly from Elford, we have spoken with your son there, he lent Brother Haluin here a strong arm to lean on when he needed it.'

'You have talked with him! And what did my son have to say, there at Elford. What had he to say of me?' He was alert and ready to hear bitter rumour of complaint and estrangement, and to swallow that grief if he must.

'Very little, and certainly nothing you could not have heard with a quiet mind. No word of your sister. He mentioned that he had left home at his father's wish, and that he could not refuse you the obedience due. We had no more than a few minutes' talk with him, by pure chance. But I saw nothing there of which you should not be glad and proud. Consider, he is barely three miles away, and against his own wish, but he keeps true to his word. There is but one thing I remember him saying,' pursued Cadfael with sudden probing intent, 'that perhaps you have a father's right to hear. He asked us, very solemnly, whether our order could provide a worthwhile life for a man – if the life he most longed for was forbidden to him.'

'No!' cried Cenred in sharp protest. 'Not that! I would not for the world he should turn his back on arms and reputation and hide himself away in the cloister. He is not made for that! A youth of such promise! Brother, this does but confirm me in what I am asking. There is no putting off what must be done. Once done, he will accept it. As long as the loss is not final he will go on hoping and hankering after the impossible. It is why I want her married, married and out of this house, before ever Roscelin enters it again.'

'I understand your reasons very well,' said Haluin, opening his hollow eyes challengingly wide, 'but it would not be right to make them reasons for a marriage, if the lady is unwilling. However hard your plight, you cannot sacrifice the one to preserve the other.'

'You mistake the case,' said Cenred without heat. 'I love my young sister, I have talked with her openly and fairly. She knows, she acknowledges, the enormity of what threatened them both, the impossibility of such a love ever coming to fruit. She wants this terrible knot severed, as truly as I do. She wants a career of honour for Roscelin because she loves him, and rather than see it blighted through her she agrees to seek refuge in marriage with another man. This has been no forced surrender. And no wanton choice, either. I have done the best I could for her, it is a match any family would welcome. Jean de Perronet is a well-endowed, well-conditioned young man of good estate. He is due here today, so you may see him for yourself. Helisende already knows him, and likes if she cannot yet love him. That may come, for he is greatly drawn to her. She has fully consented to this marriage. And de Perronet has this one inestimable advantage,' he added grimly, 'his seat is far away. He will take her home to Buckingham, out of Roscelin's sight. Out of sight, out of mind I will not say, but at least the lines of a remembered face may fade gradually over the years, as even stubborn wounds heal.'

He had become eloquent by reason of his own deep disquiet and distress, a good man concerned for the best interests of all his household. He had not remarked, as Cadfael did, the gradual blanching of Haluin's thin face, the tight and painful set of his lips, or the way his linked hands gripped together in the lap of his habit until the bones shone white through the flesh. The words Cenred had not deliberately chosen to pierce or move had their own inspired force to reopen the old wound he had come all this way to try and heal. The lines of a remembered face, surely somewhat dimmed in eighteen years, were burning into vivid life again for him. And wounds that have not ceased to fester within cannot heal until they have again broken out and been cleansed, by fire if need be.

'And you need not fear, and neither need I,' said Cenred, 'that she will not be cherished and held in high regard with de Perronet. Two years back he asked for her, and for all she would have none of him or any suitor then, he has waited his time.'

'Your lady is in agreement in this matter?' asked Cadfael.

'We have all three talked of it together. And we are agreed. Will you do it? I felt it a kind of blessing on what we intend,' said Cenred simply, 'when a priest came to my door unsummoned on the eve of the bridegroom's coming. Stay over tomorrow, Brother – Father! – and marry them.'

Haluin unlocked his contorted hands slowly, and drew breath like a man awaking in pain. In a low voice he said: 'I will stay. And I will marry them.'

'I trust I have done right,' said Haluin, when they were back in their own quarters. But it did not seem that he was asking to be confirmed in his decision, rather setting it squarely before his own eyes as a responsibility he had no intention of hedging or sharing. 'I know only too well,' he said, 'the perils of proximity, and their case is more desperate than ever was mine. Cadfael, I feel myself listening to echoes I thought had died out long ago. It is all for a purpose. Nothing is without purpose. How if I fell only to show me how far I was already fallen, and force me to make the assay to rise afresh? How if I came to life again as a cripple, to make me undertake those journeys of body and spirit that I dreaded when I was strong and whole? How if God put it into my mind to go on pilgrimage in order to become some other needy soul's miracle? Were we led to this place?'

'Driven, rather,' said Cadfael practically, remembering the blinding snow, and the small beckoning spark of the torch in the drifting dark.

'It's true, to arrive on the eve of the bridegroom's coming is very apt timing. I can but go with the burden of the day,' said Haluin, 'and hope to be led aright. These second marriages in old age, Cadfael, have sorry tangles to answer for. How can two babes playing together in the rushes of the floor know that they are aunt and nephew, and fruit forbidden? A pity that love should be spent to no end.'

'I am not sure,' said Cadfael, 'that love is ever spent for no end. Well, at least now you can be still and rest for a day or so, and all the better for it. That, at any rate, comes timely.'

And that was plainly the best use Haluin could make of this halt on the way home, since he had already tried himself very near the end of his endurance. Cadfael left him in peace, and went out to take a daylight look at this manor of Vivers. A cloudy day with a fitful wind, the air free of frost, and occasional fine drifts of rain in the air, but none that lasted long.

He walked the width of the enclave to the gate, to see the full extent of the house. There were windows in the steep roof above the solar, probably two retired rooms were available there. Haluin and his companion had been accommodated considerately on the living floor. No doubt one of those upper chambers was being prepared at this moment for the expected bridegroom. The daily bustle about the courtyard seemed everywhere to be in hand without haste or confusion; things were well ordered here.

Beyond the pale of the stockade the soft, undulating landscape extended in field and copse and sparsely treed upland, all the greens still bleached and dried with winter, but the black branches showed here and there the first nodules of the leaf-buds of spring. Faint frills of snow outlined all the hollows and sheltered places, but a gleam of sun was breaking through the low cloud, and by noon all the remnant of last night's fall would be gone.

Cadfael looked into the stables and the mews, and found both well supplied and proudly kept by servitors ready and willing to show them off to an interested visitor. In a separate stall in the kennels a hound bitch lay curled in clean straw with her six pups around her, perhaps five weeks old. He could not resist going into the dim shed to take up one of the young ones, and the dam was complacent, and welcomed admiration of her brood. The soft warmth of the small body in his arms had a smell like new bread. He was just stooping to lay the pup back among its siblings when a clear, cool voice behind him said:

'Are you the priest who is to marry me?'

And there she was in the doorway, again a shadowy form against the light, so composed, so assured that she might easily be taken for a mature and stately woman of thirty, though the fresh, light voice belonged to her proper age. The girl Helisende Vivers, not yet decked out to receive her bridegroom, but in a plain housewifely gown of dark blue wool, and with a gently steaming pail of meat and meal for the hounds in one hand.

'Are you the priest who is to marry me?'

'No,' said Cadfael, slowly straightening up from the wriggling litter and the crooning bitch. 'That is Brother Haluin. I never studied for orders. I know myself better.'

'It's the lame man, then,' she said with detached sympathy. 'I am sorry he suffers such hardship. I hope they have made him comfortable, here in our house. You do know about my marriage – that Jean comes here today?'

'Your brother has told us,' said Cadfael, watching the features of her oval face emerge softly from shadow, in every plaintive, ingenuous line testifying to her youth. 'But there are things he could not tell us,' he said, watching her intently, 'except by hearsay. Only you can tell us whether this match has your consent, freely given, or no.'

Her brief silence at that did not suggest hesitation so much as a grave consideration of the man who raised the question. Her large eyes, dauntlessly honest, embraced and penetrated, quite unafraid of being penetrated in return. If she had judged him so alien to her needs and predicament as to be unacceptable, she would have closed the encounter there and then, civilly but without satisfying what would then have been mere intrusive curiosity. But she did not.

'If we do anything freely, once we are grown,' she said, 'then yes, this I do freely. There are rules that must be kept. There are others in the world with us who have rights and needs, and we are all bound. You may tell Brother Haluin – Father Haluin I must call him – that he need have no qualms for me. I know what I am doing. No one is forcing my hand.'

'I will tell him so,' said Cadfael. 'But I think you do it for others, not for yourself.'

'Then say to him that I choose – freely – to do it for others.'

'And what of Jean de Perronet?' said Cadfael.

For one instant her firm, full lips shook. It was the one thing that still disrupted her resolute composure, that she was not being fair to the man who was to be her husband. Cenred would certainly not have told him that he was getting only a sad remainder after the heart was gone. Nor could she tell him so. The secret belonged only to the family. The only hope for this hapless pair was that love might come with time, a kind of love, better, perhaps, than many marriages ever achieve, but still far short of the crown.

'I will try,' she said steadily, 'to give him all that he is asking, all that he wants and expects. He deserves well, he shall have the best I can do.'

There was no point in saying to her that it might not be enough, she already knew that, and was uneasy about a degree of deception she could not evade. It might even be, that what had already been said here in the dimness of the kennels had re-opened a deep abyss of doubt which she had almost succeeded in sealing over. Better let well alone, where there was no possibility of rendering the load she carried any lighter.

'Well, I pray you may be blessed in all you do,' said Cadfael, and drew back out of her way. The bitch had uncoiled herself from among her puppies and was nuzzling the pail, and waving a feathered tail in hungry expectation. The ordinary business of the day goes on through births, marriages, deaths and festivals. When he looked back from the doorway the girl Helisende was stooping to fill the bitch's bowl, the heavy braid of her brown hair swinging among the scrambling litter. She did not look up, but for all that he had the feeling that she was deeply and vulnerably aware of him until he turned and walked softly away.

'You'll miss your nurseling,' said Cadfael, when Edgytha came at noon to serve food and drink for them. 'Or will you be going south with her when she's married?'

The old woman lingered, taciturn by nature but visibly in

need of unburdening a heart by no means reconciled to losing her darling. Within the stiff folds of her wimple her withered cheek trembled.

'What should I do at my age, in a strange place? I am too old to be of much value now, I shall stay here. At least I know the way of things here, and everyone knows me. What respect should I have in a strange household? But she'll go, I know that! She'll go, I suppose, as go she must. And the young man's well enough – if my lamb had not another in her eye and in her heart.'

'And one placed so far out of reach,' Haluin reminded her gently, but his own face was pale, and when she turned and looked at him in silence for a long moment he averted his eyes and turned away his head.

Her eyes were the pale, washed blue of fading harebells. Once, shadowed by lashes now grown thin and meagre, they might have resembled more the colour of periwinkles. 'So my lord will have told you,' she said. 'So they all say. And if there's no help, she might do much worse. I know! I came here in attendance on her mother, all those years ago, and that was no lover's match, neither, her so young, and him nigh on three times her age. A decent, kind man he was, but old, old! She had good need, poor lady, of someone from home, someone she knew well and could trust. At least they're marrying my girl to somebody young.'

Cadfael asked what had been preoccupying his mind for some little while, since no word had been said on the matter: 'Is Helisende's mother dead?'

'No, not dead. But she took the veil at Polesworth, it must be eight years ago now, after the old lord died. She's within your own order, a Benedictine nun. She had always a leaning towards it, and when her husband died, and she began to be talked about and bargained about as widow ladies are, and urged to marry again, rather than that she left the world. It's one way of escape,' said Edgytha, and set her lips grimly.

'And left her daughter motherless?' said Haluin, with more reproof in his voice than he intended.

'She left her daughter very well mothered! She left her to the lady Emma and to me!' Edgytha smouldered for a moment, and subdued the brief fire within lowered eyelids. 'Three mothers that child has had, and all fond. My lady Emma could never be harsh to any young thing. Too soft, indeed, the pair of them could always get their will of her. But my own lady was given to solitude and melancholy, and when it came to a new marriage, no, she would not, she took the veil gladly rather than marry again.'

'Helisende has never considered that refuge?' asked Cadfael.

'Not she, God forbid she ever should! My girl was never of that mind. For those who take to it kindly it may be bliss, but for those who are pressed into it, it must be a hell on earth! If you'll pardon my tongue, Brothers! You know your own vocation best, and no doubt you took the cowl for the best of reasons, but Helisende . . . No, I would not want that for her. Better by far this Perronet lad, if there has to be a second-best.' She had begun to gather up the platters and dishes they had emptied, and took up the pitcher to refill their cups. 'I did hear say that you've been at Elford, and seen Roscelin there. Is that true?'

'Yes,' said Cadfael, 'we left Elford only yesterday. We did, by chance, have some brief talk with the young man, but never knew until this morning that he came from this neighbouring manor of Vivers.'

'And how did he look?' she asked longingly. 'Is he well? Was he down in spirits? I have not seen him for a month or more, and I know how ill he took it that he should be sent away like some offending page from his own home, when he had done no wrong, nor thought none. As good a lad as ever stepped! What had he to say?'

'Why, he was in excellent health at any rate,' said Cadfael

115

cautiously, 'and very fair spirits, considering all. It's true he did complain of being banished, and was very ill-content where he is. Naturally he said little about the circumstances, seeing we were chance comers and unknown to him, and I daresay he would have said no more to anyone else who had as little business in the matter. But he did say he had given his word to abide by his father's orders, and wait for leave before he'd venture home.'

'But he does not know,' she said, between anger and help-lessness, 'what's being planned here. Oh, he'll get leave to come home fast enough as soon as Helisende is out of the house, and far away south on her way to that young man's manor. And what a homecoming that will be for the poor lad! Shame to deal so behind his back!'

'They think it for the best,' said Haluin, pale and moved. 'Even for his best interests, they believe. And this matter is hard even for them. If they are mistaken in hiding this marriage from him until it is over, surely they may be forgiven.'

'There are those,' said Edgytha darkly, 'who never will be.' She picked up her wooden tray, and the keys at her girdle chimed faintly as she moved towards the door. 'I wish this had been honestly done. I wish he had been told. Whether he could ever have her or not, he had a right to know, and to give his blessing or his ban. How was it you were brought in touch with him there, to know the half of his name but not the whole?'

'It was the lady mentioned his name,' said Cadfael, 'when de Clary came in from riding, and the young man was with him. Roscelin, she called him. It was later we spoke with him. He saw my friend here stiff from a night on his knees, and came to lend him an arm to lean on.'

'So he would!' she said, warming. 'To anyone he saw in need. The lady, you say? Audemar's lady?'

'No, our errand was not to him, we never saw his wife

116

and children. No, this was his mother, Adelais de Clary.'

The dishes jangled momentarily on Edgytha's tray. With care she balanced it on one hand, and reached to the latch of the door. 'She is there? There at Elford?'

'She is. Or she was when we left, yesterday, and with the snow coming so shortly after, she is surely there still.'

'She visits very rarely,' said Edgytha, shrugging. 'They say there's small love lost between her and her son's wife. That's no uncommon thing, either, I suppose, so they're just as well apart.' She nudged the door open expertly with an elbow, and swung the large tray through the doorway edgewise. 'Do you hear the horses, outside there? That will be Jean de Perronet's party riding in.'

There was nothing clandestine or secretive, certainly, about Jean de Perronet's arrival, though nothing ceremonious or showy, either. He came with one body-servant and two grooms, and with two led horses for the bride and her attendant, and pack-horses for the baggage. The entire entourage was practical and efficient, and de Perronet himself went very plainly, without flourishes in his dress or his manner, though Cadfael noted with appreciation the quality of his horseflesh and harness. This young man knew where to spend his money, and where to spare.

They had gone out, Haluin and Cadfael together, to watch the guests dismount and unload. The afternoon air was again clearing towards a night frost, but there were scudding clouds in the upper air, and might be further flurries of snow in the dark hours. The travellers would be well content to be under a sound roof and out of the chilly wind.

De Perronet dismounted from his flecked roan horse before the door of the hall, and Cenred came striding down the steps to meet him and embrace him, and lead him by the hand up to the doorway, where the lady Emma waited to welcome him as warmly. Helisende, Cadfael noted, did not appear. At supper at the high table she would have no choice but to attend, but at this stage it was fitting that the honours of the house should rest with her brother and his wife, the guardians of her person and the disposers of her marriage. Host, hostess and guest vanished within the great hall. Cenred's servants and de Perronet's grooms unloaded baggage and stabled horses, and went about the business so practically that within a matter of minutes the courtyard was empty.

So that was the bridegroom! Cadfael stood considering what he had seen, and so far could find no fault in it except that it was, as Edgytha had said, a second-best. And a second-best was all that boy would gain. A young man of perhaps twenty-five or twenty-six, already accustomed to authority and responsibility by his bearing, and well capable of handling them. His men, these favoured ones at least, were easy with him. He knew his business as they knew theirs, and there was an air of mutual respect between them. Moreover, he was a goodlooking young man, tall and shapely, of open, amiable countenance, and by the look of him in the happiest possible humour on the eve of his marriage. Cenred had done his best for his young sister, and his best promised to turn out very well. A pity it could not have been what her heart desired.

'But what else could he have done?' said Haluin, betraying in few words the depth of his own dismay and doubt.

Chapter Eight

N THE LATE afternoon Cenred sent his steward to ask the two Benedictine brothers if they felt able to join his household at supper in hall, or if Father Haluin preferred to continue his rest in retirement, and be waited on in his own chamber. Haluin, who had withdrawn into a dark, inward meditation, would certainly rather have remained apart, but felt it discourteous to absent himself any longer, and made the effort to emerge from his anxious silence, and do honour to the company at the high table. They had given him a place close to the bridal pair, by virtue of his office as the priest who was to marry them. Cadfael, seated a little apart, had them all in view. And below, in the body of the hall, the whole household assembled in its due ranks, under the glow of the torches.

It occurred to Cadfael, watching Haluin's grave face, that this would be the first time his friend had ever been called upon to be go-between for God. It was true that the young brothers were being encouraged to aim at orders, more now than ever in the past, but many of them would be, as Haluin was, priests without pastoral cares, who in a long life would probably never christen, never marry, never bury, never ordain others to follow them in the same sheltered paths. It is a terrible responsibility, thought Cadfael, who had never aspired to ordination, to have the grace of God committed to a man's hands, to be privileged and burdened to play a part in other people's lives, to promise them salvation in baptism, to lock their lives together in matrimony, to hold the key to purgatory at their departing. If I have meddled, he thought devoutly, and God knows I have, when need was and there was no better man to attempt it, at least I have meddled only as a fellow-sinner, tramping the same road, not as a vicomte of heaven, stooping to raise up. Now Haluin faces this same terrible demand, and no wonder if he is afraid.

He looked along the array of faces which Haluin, being so close beside them, could see only as overlapping profiles, each briefly seen as the ripple of movement flowed along the high table, and lit deceptively by the falling glow of the torches. Cenred's broad, open, blunt-featured countenance a little drawn and taut with strain, but resolutely jovial, his wife presiding over the table with determined amiability and a somewhat anxious smile, de Perronet in happy innocence, shining with evident pleasure at having Helisende seated beside him and all but his already. And the girl, pale and quiet and resolutely gracious at his side, doing her gallant best to respond to his brightness, since this grief was no fault of his, and she had acknowledged that he deserved better. Seeing them thus together, there was no question of the man's attachment, and if he missed the like radiance in her, perhaps he accepted that as the common ground on which marriages begin, and was ready and willing to be patient until the bud came to flower.

This was the first time Haluin had seen the girl since she had startled him to his feet here in the hall, and brought him down in that crashing fall, half-dazed as he already was by the stinging wind and the blinding snow. And this stiff young figure in her best, gilded by the torchlight, might have been a stranger, never before seen. He looked at her, when chance brought her profile into clear view, with doubt and bewilderment, burdened by a responsibility new to him, and heavy to bear.

It was late when the women withdrew from the high table, leaving the men to their wine, though they would not sit here in hall much longer. Haluin looked round to catch Cadfael's eye, agreeing in a glance that it was time for them to leave host and guest together, and Haluin was already reaching for his crutches and bracing himself for the effort of rising, when Emma came in again from the solar with a flustered step and an anxious face, a young maidservant at her heels.

'Cenred, here's something strange happened! Edgytha is gone out and has not returned, and now it's beginning to snow again, and where should she be going, thus in the night? I sent for her to attend me to bed, as always, and she's nowhere to be found, and now Madlyn here says that she went out hours ago, as soon as it was dusk.'

Cenred was slow to turn his mind from his hospitable duty towards his guest to an apparently small domestic problem, surely the women's business rather than his.

'Why, Edgytha may surely go out if she so chooses,' he said good-humouredly, 'and will come back when she chooses no less. She's a free woman, knows her own mind, and can be trusted to mind her duties. If she's once missing when she's called for, that's no great matter. Why should you worry over it?'

'But when does she ever do so without saying? Never! And now it's snowing again, and she's been gone four hours or more, if Madlyn says true. How if she's come to harm? She would not stay away so long of her own will. And you know how I value her. I would not for the world that any harm should come to her.'

121

'No more would I,' said Cenred warmly, 'nor to any of my people. If she's gone astray we'll look for her. But no need to fret before we know of any mishap. Here, girl, speak up, what is it you know of the matter? You say she went out some hours ago?'

'Sir, so she did!' Madlyn came forward willingly, wide-eyed with half-pleasurable excitement. 'It was after we'd made all ready. I was coming in from the dairy, and I saw her come forth from the kitchen with her cloak about her, and I said to her that this was like to be a busy night, and she'd be missed, and she said she'd be back before she was called for. It was just beginning to get dark then. I never thought she'd be gone so long.'

'And did you not ask her where she was going?' demanded Cenred.

'I did,' said the girl, 'though it was little enough she was ever likely to tell about her own business, and I should have known she'd make a sour answer if she made any at all. But there's no sense to be made of it. She said she was going to find a cat,' said Madlyn in baffled innocence, 'to put among the pigeons.'

If it meant nothing to her, it had a meaning for Cenred and for his wife, who plainly heard it now for the first time. Emma's startled gaze flew to her husband's face as he came abruptly to his feet. The look they exchanged Cadfael could read as if he had the words ringing in his ears. He had been given clues enough to make the reading easy. Edgytha was nurse to them both, indulged them, loved them like her own, resents even their separation, whatever the church and the ties of blood may say, and much more this marriage that makes the separation final. She is gone to enlist help to prevent what she deplores, even at this last moment. She is gone to tell Roscelin what is being done behind his back. She is gone to Elford.

None of which could be said aloud, here in front of Jean

de Perronet, who stood now at Cenred's side, looking from face to face round the circle, puzzled and sympathetic in a domestic trouble which was none of his business. An old servant gone missing in the evening, with night coming on and snow falling, called for at least a token search. He made the suggestion ingenuously, filling a silence which at any moment might have caused him to look more narrowly at what was happening here.

'Should we not look for her, if she's been gone so long? The ways are not always safe at night, and for a woman venturing alone . . .'

The diversion came as a blessing, and Cenred seized on it gratefully. 'So we will. I'll send out a party by the most likely way. It may be she's only been delayed by the snow, if she intended a visit in the village. But this need not give you any concern, Jean. I would not wish your stay to be marred. Leave this matter to my men, we have enough in the household. And rest assured she cannot be far, we shall soon find her and see her safe home.'

'I will gladly come out with you,' de Perronet offered.

'No, no, I will not have it. Let all things here go as we have planned them, and nothing spoil the occasion. Use my house as your own, and take your night's rest with a quiet mind, for tomorrow this small flurry will be over and done.'

It was not difficult to persuade the helpful guest to abandon his generous intention, perhaps it had been made only as a courteous gesture. A man's household affairs are his, and best left to him. It is civil to offer help, but wise to give way gracefully. Cenred knew very well now where Edgytha had set out to go, there would be no question of which road to take in hunting for her. Moreover, there was some genuine call for concern, for in four hours she could have been there and back even in snow. Cenred quit his supper-table purposefully, driving the men of his following before him to muster within the hall door. He bade de Perronet an emphatic goodnight, which was accepted pliantly as dismissal even from this domestic conference, and issued brisk orders to those of his servants whom he chose to go with the search party, six of the young and vigorous and his steward with them.

'What must we do?' Brother Haluin wondered half-aloud, standing with Cadfael a little apart.

'You,' said Cadfael, 'must go to your bed, like a sensible man, and sleep if you can. And a prayer or two will not come amiss. I am going with them.'

'Along the nearest road to Elford,' said Haluin heavily.

'To find a cat to put among the pigeons. Yes, where else? But you stay here. There is nothing you could do or say, if there has to be speech, that I cannot.'

The hall door was opened, the party tramped down the steps into the courtyard, two of them carrying torches. Cadfael, following last, looked out upon a glittering, frosty night. The ground was covered but meagrely, small, needle-sharp flakes out of an almost clear sky, brittle with stars and too cold for a heavy fall. He looked back from the doorway, and saw the women of the house, gentlefolk and servants alike, drawn together in mutual uneasiness in the far corner of the hall, all eyes following their departing menfolk, the maids huddling close, Emma with her smooth, gentle face wrung in distress, and pulling nervously at her plump fingers.

And Helisende standing a pace apart, the only one not clinging to her kind for comfort. She was far enough back from one of the sconces for the torchlight to show her face fully, without exaggerated shadows. All that Emma had reported to her husband, all that Madlyn had told, Helisende surely knew now. She knew where Edgytha was gone, she knew for what purpose. She was staring wide-eyed into a future she could no longer foretell, where the

124

results of this night's work hid themselves in bewilderment and dismay and possible catastrophe. She had prepared herself for a willing sacrifice, but she found herself utterly unprepared for whatever threatened now. Her face seemed as still and composed as ever, yet it had lost all its calm and certainty, her resolution had become helplessness, and her resignation changed to desperation. She had arrived at an embattled ground she believed she could hold, at whatever cost to herself, and now that ground shook and parted under her feet, and she was no longer in control of her own fate. The image of her shattered gallantry, disarmed and vulnerable, was the last glimpse Cadfael carried out with him into the darkness and the frost.

Cenred drew his cloak close about his face against the wind, and set out from the gate of the manor on a path that was strange to Cadfael. With Haluin he had turned in from the distant highway, straight towards the gleam of light from the manor torches, but this way slanted back to strike the road much nearer to Elford, and would probably cut off at least half a mile of the distance. The night had its own lambent light, partly from the stars, partly from the thin covering of snow, so that they were able to go quickly, spread out in a line centred upon the path. The country here was open, at first bare of trees, then threading a belt of woods and scrubland. They heard nothing but their own footsteps and breath, and the soft whining of the wind among the bushes. Twice Cenred halted them to have silence, and called aloud to the night, but got no answer.

For one who knew this path well, Cadfael calculated, the distance to Elford would be roughly two miles. Edgytha could have been back in Vivers long ago, and by what she had said to the maid Madlyn she had intended to return in ample time to be at her mistress's disposal after supper. Nor could she have strayed from a known way on so bright a night, and in barely more than a sprinkling of snow. It began to seem clear to him that something had happened to prevent either her errand, or her safe return from it. Not the rigours of nature or the caprice of chance, but the hand of man. And on such a night those outcast creatures who preyed upon travellers, even if any such existed here in this open country, were unlikely to be out and about their dark business, since their prey would hardly be eager to venture out in such a frost. No, if any man had intervened to prevent Edgytha from reaching her goal, it was with deliberate intent. There was, perhaps, one better possibility, that if she had reached Roscelin with her news, he had persuaded her not to return, but to remain at Elford in safety and leave the rest to him. But Cadfael was not sure that he believed in that. If it had happened so, Roscelin would already have been striding indignantly into the hall at Vivers before ever Edgytha had been missed from her place.

Cadfael had drawn close alongside Cenred, pressing forward in haste in the centre of his line of hunters, and one dark, sidelong glance saluted and recognised him, without great surprise. 'There was no need, Brother,' said Cenred shortly. 'We are enough for the work.'

'One more will do no harm,' said Cadfael.

No harm, but possibly none too welcome. As well if this matter could be kept strictly private to the Vivers household. Yet it seemed that Cenred was not greatly troubled by the presence of a chance Benedictine monk among his search party. He was intent on finding Edgytha, and preferably before she reached Elford, or failing that, in time to negate whatever mischief she had set afoot. Perhaps he expected to meet his son somewhere along the way, coming in haste to prevent that marriage that would destroy his last vain hopes. But they had gone somewhat more than a mile, and the night remained empty about them.

They were moving through thin, open woodland, over

tufted, uneven grass, where the frozen snow lay too lightly to flatten the blades to earth, and they might have passed by the slight hummock beside the path on the right hand but for the dark ground that showed through the covering of white lace, darker than the bleached brown of the wintry turf. Cenred had passed it by, but checked sharply when Cadfael halted, and stared down as he was staring.

'Quickly, bring the torch here close!'

The yellow light outlined clearly the shape of a human body lying sprawled, head away from the path, whitened over with a crust of snow. Cadfael stooped and brushed away the crystalline veil from an upturned face, open-eyed and contorted in astonished fright, and a head of grey hair from which the hood had fallen back as she fell. She lay on her back but inclined towards her right side, her arms flung up and wide as if to ward off a blow. Her black cloak showed darkly through the filigree of white. Over her breast a small patch marred the veil, where her blood, in a meagre flow, had thawed the flakes as they fell. There was no telling immediately, from the way she lay, whether she had been on her way outward or homeward when she was struck down, but it seemed to Cadfael that at the last moment she had heard someone stealing close behind her, and whirled about with hands flung up to protect her head. The dagger her attacker had meant to slip between her ribs from behind had missed its stroke, and been plunged into her breast instead. She was dead and cold, the frost confounding all conjecture as to when she must have died.

'God's pity!' said Cenred on a whispering breath. 'This I never thought to see! Whatever she intended, why this?'

'Wolves hunt even in frost,' said his steward heavily. 'Though what rich traffic there can be for them here heaven knows! And see, there's nothing taken, not even her cloak. Masterless men would have stripped her.'

Cenred shook his head. 'There are none such in these

parts, I swear. No, this is a different matter. I wonder, I wonder which way she was bound when she was struck dead!'

'When we move her,' said Cadfael, 'we may find out. What now? There's nothing now can be done for her. Whoever used the knife knew his grim business, it needed no second stroke. And whatever footprints he left behind the ground's too hard to show, even where the snow has not covered them.'

'We must carry her home,' said Cenred sombrely. 'And a sorry matter that will be for my wife and sister. They set great store by the old woman. She was always loyal and trustworthy, all these years since my young stepmother brought her into the household. This must not pass without requital! We'll send ahead to see if she ever came to Elford, and what's known of her there, and whether they have any word of chance marauders haunting these ways, perhaps on the run from other regions. Though that's hard to believe. Audemar keeps a firm hand on his lands.'

'Shall we send back and fetch a litter, my lord?' asked the steward. 'She's but a light weight, we could make shift to carry her back in her cloak.'

'No, no need to make another journey. But you, Edred, you take Jehan here with you, and go on to Elford, and find out what's known of her there, if anyone has met and spoken with her. No, take two men with you. I would not have you in any danger on the road, if there are masterless men abroad.'

The steward accepted his orders, and took one of the torches to light him the rest of the way. The small, resiny spark dwindled along the pathway towards Elford, and vanished gradually into the night. Those remaining turned to the body, and lifted it aside to unfasten and spread out on the path the cloak she wore. As soon as she was raised one thing at least was made plain.

'There's snow under her,' said Cadfael. The shrunken shape of her was dark and moist where contact had been close enough for her body's lingering warmth to melt the flakes, but all round the rim where the folds of her clothing had lain only lightly, a worn border of lace remained. 'It was after the snow began that she fell. She was on her way home.'

She was light and limp in their hands. The chill of her body was from frost, not rigor. They wound her closely in her cloak, and bound her safely with two or three belts and Cadfael's rope girdle, to give hand-holds for the servants who carried her, and so they bore her back the mile or so they had come, to Vivers.

The household was still awake and aware, unable to rest until they knew what was happening. One of the maids saw the lamentable little procession entering at the gate, and ran wailing to tell Emma. By the time they brought Edgytha's body up into the hall the whole fluttered dovecote of maids was again assembled, huddled together for comfort. Emma took charge with more resolution than might have been expected from her soft and gentle person, and swept the girls into service with a briskness that kept them from tears, preparing a trestle table in one of the small chambers for a bier, composing the disordered limbs, heating water, bringing scented linen from the chests in the hall to drape and cover the dead. The funeral ceremonies do as much for the living as for the dead, in occupying their hands and minds, and consoling them for things left undone or badly done during life. Very shortly the murmur of subdued voices from the death-chamber had softened from distress and dismay into a gentle, almost soothing elegiac crooning.

Emma came out into the hall, where her husband and his men were warming their chilled feet at the fire, and rubbing the sense back into their numbed hands.

129

'Cenred, how is this possible? Who could have done such a thing?'

No one attempted to answer that, nor had she looked for an answer.

'Where did you find her?'

That her husband did answer, scrubbing wearily at his furrowed forehead. 'Past the halfway to Elford by the short road, lying beside the path. And she'd been there no long time, for there was snow under her. It was on her way back here that someone struck her down.'

'You think,' said Emma in a low voice, 'she had been to Elford?'

'Where else by that path? I've sent Edred on there, to find out if she came, and who has spoken with her. In an hour or so they should be back, but whether with any news, God alone knows.'

They were both of them moving delicately about and about the heart of the matter, avoiding the mention of Roscelin's name, or any word of the reason why Edgytha should go rushing out alone on a wintry night. True, word had gone round even in the kennels and mews by then, and the entire household of Vivers was gathering uneasily, the indoor servants hovering in an anxious group in the corners of the hall, those from without prowling and peering over their shoulders, unable to withdraw to their own proper business or their normal rest until something should happen within here to scatter them. Few of all these, if any, could be in their lord's confidence in the matter of Roscelin's outlawed love, but many of them might have guessed at the undercurrents sweeping Helisende into this hasty marriage. Some reserve in speech would have to be observed in front of all this clan.

And here, to complicate matters further, came Jean de Perronet from the chamber above, where he had retired out of courtesy, but not to sleep, for he was still in his supper-

130

table finery. And here, too, was Brother Haluin from his bed, anxious and silent. All those under the roof of Vivers that night had been drawn gradually and almost stealthily into the hall.

No, not quite all. Cadfael looked round the assembly, and missed one face. Where all others foregathered, Helisende absented herself.

By the look of his face de Perronet had been doing some serious thinking since he bowed to his host's wish, and let the search party go out into the night without him. He came into the hall with a face composed and grave, revealing nothing of what went on in his mind, took his time about looking all round the mute and dour circle of them, and looked last and longest at Cenred, who stood with his boots steaming in the ashes of the hearth, and his head bent to stare blankly into the embers of the fire.

'I think,' said de Perronet with deliberation, 'this has not ended well. You have found your maidservant?'

'We have found her,' said Cenred.

'Misused? Dead? Do you tell me you have found her dead?'

'And not of cold! Stabbed to death,' said Cenred bluntly, 'and left by the wayside. And no sign of another soul have we seen or heard along the road, though this befell no long time ago, after the snow began to fall.'

'Eighteen years she has been with us,' said Emma, wringing her hands together wretchedly under her breast. 'Poor soul, poor soul, to end like this – struck down by some outlaw vagabond to die in the cold. I would not for the world have had this happen!'

'I am sorry,' said de Perronet, 'that such a thing should be, and at such a time as this. Can there be some link between the occasion that brought me here, and this woman's death?'

'No!' cried husband and wife together, rather resisting

the thought already in their minds than lying to deceive the guest. 'No,' said Cenred more softly, 'I pray there is not, I trust there is not. It is of all chances the most unhappy, yet surely no more than chance.'

'There are such unblessed chances,' admitted de Perronet, but with evident reserve. 'And they do not spare to mar festivals, even marriages. You do not wish to put off this one beyond tomorrow?'

'No, why so? It is our grief, not yours. But it is murder, and I must send to the sheriff, and loose a hunt for the murderer. She has no living kin that I know of, it is for us to bury her. What's needful we shall do. It need not cast a shadow upon you.'

'I fear it already has,' said de Perronet, 'upon Helisende. The woman, I believe, was her nurse, and dear to her.'

'The more reason you should take her away from here, to a new home and a new life.' He looked round for her then for the first time, startled not to find her there among the women, but relieved that she was not there to complicate a matter already vexed enough. If she had indeed been able to fall asleep, so much the better, let her sleep on, and know nothing worse until morning. The maidservants were drifting back from the room where they had been busy making Edgytha's body seemly. There was nothing more they could do here, and their uneasy presence, mute and fearful in hovering groups, became oppressive. Cenred stirred himself with an effort to be rid of them.

'Emma, send the women to their beds. There's no more to be done here, and they need not wait. And you, fellows, be off and get your sleep. All's done that can be done till Edred gets back from Elford, no need for the whole household to wait up for him.' And to de Perronet he said: 'I sent him on with two others of my men to inform my overlord of this death. Murder in these parts is within his writ, this will be his business no less than mine. Come, Jean, with your

132

leave we'll withdraw to the solar, and leave the hall to the sleepers.'

Doubtless, thought Cadfael, watching the harassed lines of Cenred's face, he would be happier if de Perronet chose to draw off once again from all involvement, and stand apart, but there's no chance of that now. And however he hedges round the truth of why his steward has pushed on to Elford, the very name of that place has now assumed a significance there's no evading. And this is not a man who likes deception, or practises it with pleasure or skill.

The women had accepted their orders at once, and dispersed, still whispering and fearful, to their quarters. The menservants quenched the torches, leaving only two by the great door to light the way in, and fed and damped down the fire to burn slowly through the night. De Perronet followed his host to the door of the solar, and there Cenred, turning, waved Cadfael to join them within.

'Brother, you were a witness, you can testify to how we found her. It was you showed how the snow had begun to fall before she was struck down. Will you wait with us, and see what word my steward brings back with him?'

There was no word said as to whether Brother Haluin should consider this invitation as applying equally to him, but he caught Cadfael's eye, deprecating rather than recommending such a move, and chose rather to ignore it. Enough had already happened to exercise his mind, if he was to join two people whose imminent marriage was at least suspect of bringing about a death. He needed to know what lay behind these nocturnal wanderings, and withdraw from his commitment if he saw reason. He set his lips, and followed the company into the solar, his crutches heavy and slow in the rushes, and starting a dull echo as he stepped on to the floorboards within. He took his seat on a bench in the dimmest corner, an unobtrusive listener, as Cenred sat down wearily at the table, and spread his elbows on the board, propping his head between muscular hands.

'Your men are on foot?' asked de Perronet.

'Yes.'

'Then we may have a long wait yet before they can be here again. Had you other parties out on other roads?'

Cenred said starkly: 'No,' and offered no further words by way of explanation or excuse. Not a quarter of an hour ago, thought Cadfael, watching, he would have evaded that, or left it unanswered. Now he is gone beyond caring for discretion. Murder brings out into the open many matters no less painful, while itself still lurking in the dark.

De Perronet shut his lips and clenched his teeth on any further questioning, and set himself to wait in uncommitted patience. The night had closed in on the manor of Vivers in hushed stillness, ominous and oppressive. Doubtful if anyone in the hall slept, but if any of them moved it was furtively, and if any spoke it was in whispers.

Nevertheless, the wait was not to be as long as de Perronet had prophesied. The silence was abruptly shivered by the thudding of galloping hooves on the hard-frozen earth of the courtyard, a furious young voice yelling peremptorily for service, the frantic running of grooms without, and the hasty stirring of all the wakeful retainers within. Feet ran blindly in the dark, stumbling and rustling in the rushes, flint and steel spat sparks too brief and hasty to catch the tinder, the first torch was plunged into the turfed-down fire, and carried in haste to kindle others. Before the listeners in the solar could burst out into the hall a fist was thumping at the outer door, and an angry voice demanded entry.

Two or three ran to unbar, knowing the voice, and were sent reeling as the heavy door was flung back to the wall, and into the brightening flurry of torchlight burst the figure of Roscelin, head uncovered, flaxen hair on end from the speed of his ride, blue eyes blazing. The cold of the night blew in with him, and all the torches guttered and smoked, as Cenred, erupting out of the solar, was halted as abruptly on the threshold of the hall by his son's fiery glare.

'What is this Edred tells me of you?' demanded Roscelin. 'What have you done behind my back?'

Chapter Nine

OR ONCE paternal authority was caught at a disadvantage, and Cenred was all too aware of it. Nor had he the past reputation of a family tyrant to fall back on, but he did his best to wrest back the lost initiative.

'What are you doing here?' he demanded sternly. 'Did I send for you? Did your lord dismiss you? Has either of us released you from your bond?'

'No,' said Roscelin, glittering. 'I have no leave from any man, and have not asked for any. And as for my bond, you loosed me from it when you played me false. It's not I who have broken faith. And as for the duty I owe to Audemar de Clary, I'll return to it if I must, and abide whatever his displeasure visits on me, but not until you render me account here openly of what you intended in the dark behind my back. I listened to you, I owned you right, I obeyed you. Did you owe me nothing in return? Not even honesty?'

Another father might well have felled him for such insolence, but Cenred had no such option. Emma was plucking anxiously at his sleeve, troubled for both her menfolk. De Perronet, alert and grim, loomed at his shoulder, eyeing the

137

enraged boy confronting them, and already apprised of an inevitable threat to his own plans. What else could have brought this youngster haring through the night? And by all the signs he had come by the shortest road, dangerous in the dark, or he could not have arrived so soon. Nothing that had happened this night was accident or chance. The marriage of Helisende Vivers had brought about all this coil of murder and search and pursuit, and what more was to come of it there was as yet no knowing.

'I have done nothing,' said Cenred, 'of which I need to be ashamed, and nothing for which I need account to you. Well you know what your own part must be, you have agreed to it, do not complain now. I am the master in my own house, I have both rights and duties towards my family. I will discharge them as I see fit. And for the best!'

'Without the courtesy of a word to me!' flared Roscelin, burning up like a stirred fire. 'No, I must hear it only from Edred, after the damage has already begun, after a death that can surely be laid at your own door. Was that for the best? Or dare you tell me Edgytha is dead for some other cause, by some stranger's hand? That's mischief enough, even if it's no worse than that. But whose plans sent her out into the night? Dare you tell me she was on some other errand? Edred says she was on her way to Elford when someone cut her off. I am here to prevent the rest.'

'Your son refers, as I suppose,' said de Perronet, loudly and coldly, 'to the marriage arranged between the lady Helisende and me. In that matter, I think, I too have a say.'

Roscelin's wide blue stare swung from his father's face to the guest's. It was the first time he had looked at him, and the encounter held him silent for a long moment. They were not strangers to each other, Cadfael recalled. The two families were acquainted, perhaps even distant kin, and two years ago de Perronet had made a formal offer for Helisende's hand. There was no personal animosity in

Roscelin's glare, rather a baffled and frustrated rage against circumstance than against this favoured suitor, to whom he could not and must not be a rival.

'*You* are the bridegroom?' he said bluntly.

'I am, and will maintain my claim. And what have you to urge against it?'

Animosity or not, they had begun to bristle like fighting cocks, but Cenred laid a restraining hand on de Perronet's arm, and frowned his son back with a forbidding gesture.

'Wait, wait! This has gone too far now to be left in the dark. Do you tell me, boy, that you heard of this marriage, as you heard of Edgytha's death, only from Edred?'

'How else?' demanded Roscelin. 'He came puffing in with his news and roused the household, Audemar and all. Whether he meant me to hear when he blurted out word of this marriage I doubt, but I did hear it, and here am I to find out for myself what you never meant me to question. And we shall see if all is being done for the best!'

'Then you had not seen Edgytha? She never reached you?'

'How could she if she was lying dead a mile or more from Elford?' demanded Roscelin impatiently.

'It was after the snow that she died. She had been some hours gone, long enough to have reached Elford and been on her way back. *Somewhere* she had been, from somewhere she was certainly returning. Where else could it have been?'

'So you thought she had indeed reached Elford, said Roscelin slowly. 'I never heard but that she was dead, I thought it was on her way. On her way to me! Is that what you had in mind? To warn me of what was being done here in my absence?'

Cenred's silence and Emma's unhappy face were answer enough.

'No,' he said slowly, 'I never saw hide or hair of her. Nor

did anyone in Audemar's household as far as I know. If she ever was there at all, I don't know to whom she came. Certainly not to me.'

'Yet it could have been so,' said Cenred.

'It was not so. She did not come. Nevertheless,' said Roscelin relentlessly, 'here am I as if she had, having heard it from another mouth. God knows I am grieved for Edgytha, but what is there now to be done for her but bury her with reverence, and after, if we can, find and bury her murderer? But it is not too late to reconsider what was intended here for tomorrow, it is not too late to change it.'

'I marvel,' said Cenred harshly, 'that you do not charge me outright with this death.'

Roscelin was brought up short against an idea so monstrous, and stood open-mouthed with shock, his unclenched hands dangling childishly. Plainly such a notion had never entered his ingenuous head. He stammered a furious, half-inarticulate disclaimer, and abandoned it halfway to turn again upon de Perronet.

'But you – *you* had cause enough to want her stopped, if you knew she was on her way to warn me. *You* had good cause to want her silenced, so that no voice should be raised against your marriage, as now I raise mine. Was it you who did her to death on the way?'

'This is foolery,' said de Perronet with disdain. 'Everyone here knows that I have been here in plain view all the evening.'

'So you may have been, but you have men who may be used to do your work for you.'

'Every man of whom can be vouched for by your father's household. Also, you have been told already it was not on the outward way this woman was killed, but returning. What purpose would that have served for me? And now may I ask of you, father and son both,' he demanded sharply, 'what interest has this boy in his close kinswoman's marriage, that he dares to challenge either her brother's rights or her husband's?'

Now, thought Cadfael, it is all as good as out, though no one will say it plainly. For de Perronet has wits sharp enough to have grasped already what particular and forbidden passion really drives this unhappy boy. And now it depends on Roscelin whether a decent face is kept on the affair or not. Which is asking a lot of a young man torn as he is, and outraged by what he feels as a betrayal. Now we shall see his mettle.

Roscelin had blanched into a fixed and steely whiteness, his fine bones of cheek and jaw outlined starkly in the torchlight. Before Cenred could draw breath to assert his dominance, his son had done it for him.

'My interest is that of a kinsman close as a brother life-long, and desiring Helisende's happiness beyond anything else in the world. My father's right I never have disputed, nor do I doubt he wishes her well as truly as I do. But when I hear of a marriage planned in haste and in my absence, how can I be easy in mind? I will not stand by and see her hustled into a marriage that may not be to her liking. I will not have her forced or persuaded against her will.'

'This is no such matter,' protested Cenred hotly. 'She is not being forced, she has consented willingly.'

'Then why was I to be kept in ignorance? Until the thing was done? How can I believe what your own proceedings deny?' He swung round upon de Perronet, his blanched face arduously controlled. 'Sir, against you I have no malice. I did not even know who was to be her husband. But you must see how hard it is to believe that all has been done fairly, when it has not been done openly.'

'It is in the open now,' said de Perronet shortly. 'What hinders but you should hear it from the lady's own lips? Will that content you?'

Roscelin's white face tightened yet more painfully, and

for a moment he struggled visibly against his fear of inevitable rejection and loss. But he had no choice but to agree.

'If she tells me this is her choice, then I am silenced.' He did not say that he would therefore be content.

Cenred turned to his wife, who all this while had clung loyally to her husband's side, while her troubled eyes never left her son's tormented face.

'Go and call Helisende. She shall speak for herself.'

In the heavy and uneasy silence after Emma had departed it was not clear to Cadfael whether any or all of this disturbed household had found it as strange as he did that Helisende should not long ago have come down, to discover for herself the meaning of all these nocturnal comings and goings. He could not get out of his mind the last glimpse he had had of her, standing solitary among so many, suddenly lost and confounded on a road she had believed she could walk to the end with resolute dignity. In a situation so grimly changed she had lost her bearings. A wonder, though, that she had not, in defence of her own integrity, come down with the rest to discover the best or the worst when the searchers returned. Did she even know yet that Edgytha was dead?

Cenred had advanced into the half-lit hall, abandoning even the seclusion of the solar, since there was no longer any privacy to be found behind a closed door. A woman of the household had been killed. A lady of the family found her marriage the occasion of conflict and death. There was no possibility here of any separation between master and man, or mistress and maid. They waited with equal disquiet. All but Helisende, who absented herself still.

Brother Haluin had drawn back into the shadows, and sat mute and still on a bench against the wall, hunched stiffly between the crutches he hugged to his sides. His hollow dark eyes passed intently from face to face, reading

142

and wondering. If he felt weariness, he gave no sign. Cadfael would have liked to send him away to his bed, but there hung on everyone here a compulsion so strong that there could be no departure. Only one had resisted the pull. Only one had escaped.

'What keeps the women?' fretted Cenred, as the moments dragged by. 'Does it take so long to pull on a gown?'

But it was long minutes more before Emma reappeared in the doorway, her round, gentle face full of consternation and dismay, her linked hands playing agitatedly at her girdle. Behind her the maid Madlyn peered warily, round-eyed. But of Helisende there was no sign.

'She is gone,' said Emma, too shaken and bewildered to make many words of it. 'She is not in her bed, not in her chamber, nowhere to be found in all this house. Her cloak is gone. Jehan has been out to the stables. Her saddle-horse and harness are gone with her. While you were absent she has saddled up for herself and ridden away secretly, alone.'

For once they were all alike silenced, brother, bridegroom, frustrated lover and all. While they schemed and agonised and wrangled over her fate she had taken action and fled them all. Yes, even Roscelin, for he stood stricken and amazed, utterly at a loss like all the rest. Cenred might stiffen and frown at his son, de Perronet swing round upon him in black suspicion, but plainly Roscelin had had no part in this panic flight. Even before Edgytha's death, thought Cadfael, her secret errand and failure to return had shattered all Helisende's arduously assembled certainty. Yes, de Perronet was a decent man and an honourable match, and she had pledged herself to him to remove herself from Roscelin's path, and deliver herself and him from an unbearable situation. But if that sacrifice was to bring only anger, danger and conflict, even short of death, then all was changed. Helisende had drawn back from the brink, and cut herself free.

'She has run!' said Cenred on a gusty breath, not questioning, accepting. 'How could she do it, all unseen? And when can she have set out? Where were her maids? Was there never a groom about the stable to question her going, or at least give us warning?' He passed a helpless hand over his face, and looked round darkly at his son. 'And where would she run but to you?'

It was out now, and there was no taking it back.

'Have you hidden her away somewhere in secret, and ridden here with your false indignation to cover up the sin?'

'You cannot believe that!' said Roscelin, outraged. 'I have not seen her, nor had any word from her, nor sent her any, and you know it. I'm newly ridden from Elford by that same way your men came there, and if she had been on that path we should have met. Do you think I would then have let her go anywhere alone in the night, whether on to Elford or back here? If we had met we should have been together now – wherever that might be.'

'There is a safer way by the highroad,' said de Perronet. 'Longer, but as fast on horseback, and safer going. If she did indeed set out for Elford, she may have ridden that way. She would hardly risk the same path your men had taken.'

His voice was dry and cold, and his face set in forbidding lines, but he was a practical man, and intended wasting no energy or passion on a green boy's mistaken affections. They did not threaten his position. The match he desired was arranged and accepted, and need not and would not be abandoned. What mattered now was to recover the girl unharmed.

'So she may,' agreed Cenred, encouraged. 'So most likely she would. If she reaches Elford she'll be safe enough there. But we'll send after her by the highroad, and leave nothing to chance.'

'I'll ride back by that way,' offered Roscelin eagerly, and

was off towards the door of the hall with a bound, if de Perronet had not plucked him back sharply by the sleeve.

'No, not you! What we might see of either of you again, if once you met, I much mistrust. Let Cenred seek his sister, and I'm content she'll come back to speak her own mind when all this coil is over. And when she does, boy, you had best abide it, and keep your tongue within your teeth.'

Roscelin did not like being handled, nor much savour being called 'boy' by a man whose height and reach he could match, if not his years and assurance. He wrenched his arm free strongly, and stood off further affront with a blackly lowering brow.

'So Helisende be found safe and well, and let alone in very truth to speak her own mind, and not yours, sir, nor my father's, nor any other man's, overlord or priest or king or whatever he may be, I am content. And first,' he said, turning on his father between defiance and pleading, 'find her, let me see her whole and well and used with gentleness. What else matters now?'

'I am going myself,' said Cenred with reviving authority, and strode back into the solar to reclaim the cloak he had discarded.

But there was to be no more riding out from Vivers that night. Cenred had scarcely pulled on his boots again, and his grooms were no more than hoisting down saddle and harness in the stables, when there arose the purposeful stir of half a dozen horsemen riding into the courtyard, the ring of challenge and answer at the gate, the jingle of harness and dull tramping of hooves on the frozen earth.

All those within came surging to open the door and see what company this might be, so late in the night. Edred and his companions had gone on foot, and might be expected to return on foot, and here was a well-mounted troop arriving. Out went the torches into the darkness, out went Cenred,

145

with Roscelin and de Perronet hard on his heels, and several of his menservants following.

In the yard the flickering torchlight flared and guttered and flared again on the strongly-boned countenance and massive body of Audemar de Clary, as he swung himself down from the saddle and tossed his bridle to a scurrying groom. Behind him came Edred the steward and the grooms who had been sent on with him to Elford, mounted now at de Clary's charge, along with three of Audemar's own men.

Cenred came hurrying down the steps to welcome them. 'My lord,' he said, for once formal with his friend and overlord. 'I never looked to see you tonight, but you come very timely and are more than welcome. God knows we're like to be causing you trouble enough, for we have murder here, as Edred will have told you. Murder within your writ is hard to believe, but so it is.'

'So I've heard,' said Audemar. 'Come within, and let me hear the whole tale from you. There's nothing to be done now before morning.' His eye fell on the truant Roscelin as he entered the hall, recorded the boy's grim and unrepentant countenance, and acknowledged tolerantly: 'You here, lad? That at least I expected.' Clearly the deeper reason for Roscelin's banishment was no secret from Audemar, and he had a certain easy sympathy for the boy, short of indulging his folly. He clouted him hard on the shoulder as he passed, and drew him with him into the solar. Roscelin resisted the urging, gripping his lord's sleeve urgently.

'My lord, there's more to be told. Sir,' he appealed to his father passionately. 'tell him! If she did make for Elford, where can she be now? My lord, Helisende is gone, she has ridden out alone, my father believes she must have set out for Elford – because of me! But I rode here by the rough track and saw nothing of her. Has she indeed come safely to you? Put me out of this anxiety – did she go by the high-road? Is she safe at Elford now?'

'She is not!' Brought up short against this new vexation, Audemar looked sharply from son to father and back again, well aware of the tensions that plagued them. 'We have just come by the highroad and never a sign of her or any woman have we seen. One road or the other, one of us would have met with her. Come, now!' he said, sweeping Cenred along with him in his free arm. 'Let's within, the few of us, and see what knowledge we can put together, to be used with good sense tomorrow by daylight. Madam, you should take some rest, all's done that you can do before morning, and I will make myself accountable from this on. No need for you to watch out the night.'

There was no question now as to who was master here. At his bidding Emma folded her hands thankfully, shared a glance of harried affection between her husband and her son, and departed docilely to such rest as she could hope to get before dawn. Audemar looked round once from within the solar, a sweeping glance amiable enough but unmistakable in its dominance, that dismissed all further attendance. His eye lit upon the two Benedictines, waiting unobtrusively on the edge of the scene, recognised them with a nod of easy reverence for their habit, and smiled.

'Goodnight, Brothers!' said Audemar, and drew the solar door firmly closed at his back, shutting himself in with the troubled Vivers household and their aspiring kinsman.

Chapter Ten

E IS RIGHT!' said Brother Haluin, stretched on his bed in the pre-dawn twilight, wakeful still and loosed now from his long silence on the fringe of other men's chaos. 'Goodnight, Brothers, and goodbye! There will be no marriage. There can be no marriage, there is now no bride. And even if she should come back, this match cannot now go forward as if nothing had happened to cast it into such bitter doubt. When I accepted the burden – for even so it was burdensome – there was no call to question that it was for the best, grievous though it might be. There is good reason to question now.'

'I think,' said Cadfael, listening to the muted, deliberate voice, as Haluin felt his way towards a resolution, 'you are not sorry to be delivered from your promise.'

'No, I am not sorry. Sorry enough, God knows, that a woman has died, sorry that these children should suffer unhappiness without remedy. But I could not now be answerable to God for joining the girl to any man, unless I could recover the certainty I have lost. As well that she is gone, and I pray into some safe refuge. And now it only remains,' said Brother Haluin, 'for us to take our leave. We

149

no longer have any part to play here. De Clary has plainly told us so. And Cenred will be glad to see us go.'

'And you have a vow to complete, and no further cause to delay. True!' said Cadfael torn between relief and regret.

'I have delayed too long already. It is time I acknowledged,' said Haluin inflexibly, 'how small are my own griefs, and how great the part I have chosen. I made the choice for my own craven sake, now with what life I have left I will make it good for a worthier reason.'

So this journey, thought Cadfael, has not been in vain. For the first time since his flight from the world, sick with his guilt and loss, he has ventured back into the world, and found it full of pain, into which his own pain has fallen and been lost, like a raindrop in the sea. All these years he has been outwardly dutiful, keeping every scruple of the Rule, and agonised in solitude within. His true vocation begins now. Once enlightened, Haluin may well prove the stuff of which saints are made. As for me, I am unregenerate man.

For in his heart he did not want to leave Vivers, thus with nothing resolved. Everything Haluin said was true. The bride was gone, there could be no marriage, they had no excuse for remaining here any longer, nor had Cenred any further use for them. He would indeed be glad to see them go. But Cadfael would not go gladly, turning his back upon a murder unavenged, justice out of kilter, a wrong that might never be set right.

True also, Audemer de Clary was overlord here, a man of force and decision, and with such crimes as fell within his writ he must deal. There was nothing Cadfael could tell him that Cenred would not already have told him.

And what, after all, did Cadfael really know in this matter? That Edgytha had been absent several hours before she died, since there was already snow on the ground when she fell. That she must have been on her way back to Vivers, as she had intended. That she had had ample time to go as far as Elford. That she had not been robbed. The murderer had simply killed and left her, not the way of footpads living wild. If not to stop her from warning Roscelin – for that would have been credible only on the outward journey – then to stop her mouth for another reason, before ever she could get back to Vivers. Yet what connection was there between Elford and Vivers except young Roscelin's banishment to Audemar's service? What other secret to fear betrayal but that of the planned marriage?

But Edgytha had never reached Roscelin, never had speech with him, nor had she gone to Audemar or any of his household. So if she had been to Elford, why had no one there seen her? And if she had not been to Elford, where had she been?

So if it was not what he along with his host and hostess had supposed, what was the cat Edgytha had gone to find, to put among Cenred's pigeons?

And in all probability he would never learn the answers to these questions, or learn what fortune awaited the lost girl and the unhappy boy, and the elders distressed and torn with concern for both of them. A pity! But no help for it, they could no longer trespass on Cenred's disrupted family and burdened hospitality. As soon as the household was astir they must take their leave and set out for Shrewsbury. No one would miss them. And it was high time they went home.

The morning came greyly, under a sky lightly clouded over but lofty, and threatening no further falls of snow. Only a few threads and traceries of white lingered along the bases of walls and under the trees and bushes, and the frost was yielding. It would not be a bad day for travellers.

The household was up and in ferment early. Cenred's servants rolled out of their brief sleep bleary-eyed and grim, well aware that there would be no rest for them that day.

151

Whatever else had been decided in the solemn conference in the solar overnight, whatever possible asylums had been suggested as safe havens for Helisende, it was certain that Audemar would have patrols working every road in the countryside, and enquiring at every cottage, in case someone, somewhere, had seen and spoken with Edgytha, or seen anything of a solitary and furtive figure lurking along the path she had taken. They were already gathering in the courtyard, saddling up, tightening girths and waiting stoically for their orders, when Cadfael and Haluin, booted and girded for the road, presented themselves before Cenred.

He was deep in colloquy with his steward in the middle of the bustle in the hall, when they approached him, and he turned to them courteously but blankly for a moment, as if in these graver preoccupations he had forgotten he had ever before set eyes on them. Recollection came at once, but brought him no pleasure, only a gesture of hospitable compunction.

'Brothers, I ask your pardon, you have been neglected. If we have troubles here to deal with, don't let that disturb you. Use my home as your own.'

'My lord,' said Haluin, 'we owe you thanks for all your kindness, but we must be on our way. There is now no way I can serve you. There is no more haste, since there is no more secrecy. And we have duties waiting for us at home. We are come to take our leave.'

Cenred was too honest to pretend any reluctance to part with them, and made no demur. 'I have delayed your return for my own ends,' he said ruefully, 'and all to no purpose. I am sorry I ever drew you into so vexed a business. Believe me, at least, that my intent was good. And go with my goodwill. I wish you a peaceful journey.'

'And to you, sir, the safe recovery of the lady, and the guidance of God through all perplexities,' said Haluin.

Cenred did not offer horses for the first stage of the journey, as Adelais had done for the whole of it. He had need here of all the horses at his disposal. But he watched the two habited figures, the hale and the lame, make their way slowly down the steps from the hall door, Cadfael's hand at Haluin's elbow ready to support him at need, Haluin's hands, calloused now from gripping the staves of his crutches, braced and careful at every tread. In the courtyard they threaded the bustle of preparation, and drew near to the gate. Cenred took his eyes from them with relief at being rid of one complication, and turned his face doggedly if wearily upon those remaining.

Roscelin, chafing at delay, stood bridle in hand at the gate, shifting restlessly from foot to foot, and peering impatiently back for his father or Audemar to give the word to mount. He gave the two monks a preoccupied glance as they drew near, and then, warming, bade them a good morning, and even smiled through the grey distorting mask of his own anxiety.

'You're away for Shrewsbury? It's a good step. I hope you'll have easy travelling.'

'And you a blessed end to your search,' said Cadfael.

'Blessed for me?' said the boy, again clouding over. 'I don't look for it.'

'If you find her safe and well, and no man's wife until she so pleases, that's a fair measure of blessing. I doubt if you may ask for more. Not yet,' said Cadfael cautiously. 'Take the day's measure of good, and be thankful, and who knows but more may be added?'

'You talk of impossibilities,' said Roscelin implacably. 'But you mean me well, and I take it as you mean it.'

'Where will you ride first, to look for Helisende?' asked Brother Haluin.

'Some of us back to Elford, to make sure she has not slipped between us and made her way there, after all. And

153

to every manor around, for any word of her, or of Edgytha. She cannot have gone far.' He had truly grieved and been angry for Edgytha, but the 'she' that drove all others from his mind was Helisende.

They left him chafing and agonising, more restless than the horse that shifted and stamped to be off. When they looked back from outside the gate his foot was already in the stirrup, and behind him the rest of the hunters were gathering the reins and mounting. Back to Elford first, in case Helisende had slipped through their fingers, eluding the riders on both tracks, and come safe to shelter. Cadfael and Haluin must go in the opposite direction, towards the west. They had turned some way north from the highroad to reach the lights of the manor. They did not return that way, but turned due west at once, on a trodden path that skirted the manor fence. From the limit of the enclave they heard Audemar's hunters ride forth, and turned to watch them stream out from the gate and lengthen out into a long, many-coloured thread, dwindling into the east and vanishing among the trees of the first belt of woodland.

'And is that the end of it?' wondered Haluin, suddenly grieved. 'And we shall never know what comes of it all! Poor lad, and his own case beyond hope. All his comfort in this world must be to see her happy, if that will ever be possible without him. I know,' said Brother Haluin, in compassion untainted by any lingering self-pity, 'what they suffer.'

But it seemed that it was indeed over for them, and there was no sense in looking back. They set their faces towards the west, and went forward steadily on this untested path, with the rising sun behind them, casting their elongated shadows along the moist grass.

'By this way,' said Cadfael, taking his bearings thoughtfully when they halted to eat their midday bread and cheese and strip of salt bacon in the lee of a bushy bank, 'I think we shall miss Lichfield. I judge we're already passing to the north of it. No matter, we shall find a bed somewhere before nightfall.'

Meantime, the day was clear and dry, and the country through which they made their way was pleasant, but sparsely populated, and afforded them fewer human encounters than they had met with on the direct highway through Lichfield. Having had so little sleep they made no haste, but went steadily, and took whatever rests offered along the way, wherever a solitary assart provided the hospitality of a bench by the hearth, and a few minutes of neighbourly gossip in passing.

A light wind sprang up with the approach of evening, warning them it was time to look for a night's shelter. They were in country still wasted from harsh usage fifty years past. The people of these parts had not taken kindly to the coming of the Normans, and had paid the price for their obduracy. There were the relics of deserted holdings to be seen here and there, collapsing into grass and brambles, and the ruins of a mill rotting gently into its own overgrown stream. Hamlets were few and far between. Cadfael began to scan the landscape round for any sign of an inhabited roof.

An elderly man gathering firewood in a stand of old trees straightened his bent back to answer their greetings, and peered at them curiously from within his sacking hood.

'Not half a mile on, Brothers, you'll see to your right the pale of a nunnery. They're still building, it's mostly timber yet, but the church and the cloister are in stone, you can't miss it. There's but two or three holdings in the hamlet, but the sisters take in travellers. You'll get a bed there.' And he added, eyeing their black habits: 'They're of your own persuasion, it's a Benedictine house.'

'I knew of none in these parts,' said Cadfael. 'What is this house called?'

'It's like the hamlet, called Farewell. It's no more than three years old. Bishop de Clinton set it up. You'll be made welcome there.'

They thanked him, and left him to bind up and hoist his great bundle of wood, and make off for home in the opposite direction, while they went on, encouraged, towards the west.

'I remember,' said Haluin, 'hearing something of this place, or at least of the bishop's plans for a new foundation somewhere here, close to his cathedral. But I never heard the name Farewell until – do you recall? – Cenred spoke of it, that night we first came to Vivers. The only Benedictine house in these parts, he said, when he asked where we were from. We're fortunate, it's well we came this way.'

By this time, with the twilight closing in, he was beginning to flag, in spite of the easy pace they had set. They were both glad when the path brought them to a small open green flanked by three or four cottages, and they saw beyond these the long pale fence of the new abbey, and the roof of the church above it. The track led them to a modest timber gatehouse. Both the stout gate and the grille set in it were closed, but a pull at the bell sent a succession of echoes flying away into distance within, and after a few moments brought light, flying footsteps skipping towards them from within the pale.

The grille slid open, and revealed a round, rosy, youthful face beaming through at them. Wide blue eyes surveyed their habits and tonsures, and recognised kindred.

'Good even, Brothers,' said a high, girlish voice, joyously self-important. 'You're late on the road tonight. Can we offer you a roof and a rest?'

'We were about to ask it,' said Cadfael heartily. 'Can you lodge us overnight?'

'And longer if you need,' she said cheerfully. 'Men of the Order will always be welcome here. We're off the beaten

156

track, and not yet well known, and with the place still building we offer less comfort, I daresay, than some older houses, but we have room for such guests as you. Wait till I unbar the doors.'

She was about it already, they heard the bolt shot back and the latch of the wicket lifted, and then the door opened wide in exuberant welcome, and the portress waved them in.

She could not, Cadfael thought, be more than seventeen, and new in her novitiate, one of those superfluous daughters of poorly endowed small nobility for whom there was little to spare by way of dowry, and little prospect of an advantageous marriage. She was small and softly rounded, plain of face but fresh and wholesome as new bread, and blessedly she glowed with enthusiasm in her new life, with no apparent regret for the world she had left behind. The satisfaction of trusted office became her, and so did the white wimple and black cowl framing her bright and candid face.

'Have you travelled far?' she asked, viewing Haluin's laboured gait with wide-eyed concern.

'From Vivers,' said Haluin, quick in reassurance. 'It is not so far, and we have taken it gently.'

'And have you very far still to go?'

'To Shrewsbury,' said Cadfael, 'where we belong to the abbey of Saint Peter and Saint Paul.'

'It's a long way,' she said, shaking her head over them. 'You'll be needing your rest. Will you wait here in the lodge for me, till I tell Sister Ursula she has guests? Sister Ursula is our hospitaller. The lord bishop asked for two experienced elder sisters to come to us from Polesworth for a season, to instruct the novices. We are all so new, and there's so much to learn, besides all the work we have to do in the building, and the garden. And they sent us Sister Ursula and Sister Benedicta. Sit and warm yourselves but a few minutes, and

I'll be back.' And she was off, with her light, dancing step, as blithe in her cloistered calling as any of her secular sisters could have been in approaching a more worldly marriage.

'She is truly happy,' said Brother Haluin, wondering and pleased. 'No, it is not a second-best. So I have found it in the end, but she from the beginning. The sisters from Polesworth must be women of wisdom and grace, if this is their work.'

Sister Ursula the hospitaller was a tall, thin woman perhaps fifty years old, with a lined, experienced face at once serene, resigned and even mildly amused, as if she had seen and come to terms with all the vagaries of human behaviour, and nothing could now surprise or disconcert her. If the other borrowed instructress measures up to this one, Cadfael thought, these green girls of Farewell have been fortunate.

'You're warmly welcome,' said Sister Ursula, sailing briskly into the lodge with the young portress beaming at her elbow. 'The lady abbess will be happy to receive you in the morning, but you must be most in need now of food and rest and a bed, all the more if you have such a long journey before you. Come with me, there's a chamber prepared for chance comers always, and our own brothers are all the more welcome.'

She led them out from the lodge into a narrow outer court, where the church lay before them, a modest building of stone, with the traces of the continuing work, ashlar and timber, cords and scaffolding boards, stacked neatly under its walls, in token that nothing here was finished. But in only three years they had raised the church and the entire frame of the cloister, but for the south range, where only the lower floor which housed the refectory was completed.

'The bishop has provided us the labour and a generous endowment,' said Sister Ursula, 'but we shall be building for some years yet. Meantime we live simply. We want for nothing that's needful, and hanker after nothing beyond our needs. I suppose when all these timber housings are replaced in stone my work here will be done, and I should be returning to Polesworth, where I took my vows years ago, but I don't know but I'd rather stay here, if I'm offered a choice. There's something about bringing a new foundation to birth, you feel towards it as towards a child of your own body.'

The enclave fence, doubtless, would eventually be replaced by a stone wall, the wooden buildings that lined it, infirmary, domestic offices, guest-hall and storehouses, gradually rebuilt one by one. But already the glimpse they had into the cloister in passing showed that the garth had been grassed, and a shallow stone basin in the centre held water to attract the birds.

'By next year,' said Sister Ursula, 'we shall have flowers. Sister Benedicta, our best gardener at Polesworth, came here with me, the garth is her preserve. Things grow for her, birds come to her hand. That gift I never had.'

'And has Polesworth also provided you your abbess?' asked Cadfael.

'No, Bishop de Clinton brought Mother Patrice from Coventry. We two must go back to our own house when we're no longer needed here, unless, as I say, they let us remain for life. We should need the bishop's dispensation, but who knows, he may see fit to grant it.'

Beyond the cloister a small private court opened, and the guest-hall stood on the further side of it, close to the pale fence. The small room that awaited the first travellers was dim and full of the warmth and fragrance of wood, furnished simply with two beds and a little table, with a crucifix on the wall and a prayer-desk below it.

'Use it as your domain,' said Sister Ursula cheerfully, 'and I'll have supper brought to you here. You come too late for Vespers, but if you please to join us at Compline later, you'll hear the bell. Use our church for prayer as you wish. It is but young yet, the more good souls it harbours under its roof, the better. And now, if you have all you need, I'll leave you to your rest.'

In the blessed virginal quiet of this new abbey of Farewell Brother Haluin fell rapturously asleep as soon as he returned from Compline, and slept like a child all through the night and deep into the dawn of a soft, clear morning, free of any touch of frost. He awoke to find Cadfael already up, and preparing to go and recite the morning office and offer his private prayers in the church.

'Has the bell sounded for Prime?' asked Haluin, rising in haste.

'No, nor will for half an hour yet, by the light. We can have the church to ourselves for a while, if you're so minded.'

'A good thought,' said Haluin, and went with him gladly, out into the small court, and across it to the south door into the cloister. The turf in the garth was moist and green, the bleached pallor of winter vanished overnight. The shy mist of buds that had barely showed a few days ago along the branches of the trees now had a positive colour, grown into a tender green veil. It wanted only a few more such mild days and a glimpse of the sun, and suddenly it would be spring. In the clear shallow water in the stone bowl small birds were fluttering and shrilling, aware of change. Brother Haluin approached the little church of Farewell through evidences of hope. Certainly this first church would be enlarged or replaced later, when the abbey's immediate building needs were met, its endowment assured, and its prestige established. Yet this first edifice, small and plain as it was, would always be remembered with affection, and its supplanting a matter of regret to those, like Sister Ursula and Sister Benedicta, who had been present and served at its birth.

They said the office together in the dim, stony quietness, kneeling before the small spark of the altar lamp, and made their private prayers in silence afterwards. The light softened and brightened over them, the first veiled ray of the rising sun stole through the pales of the enclave and touched the upper stones of the eastern wall into pale rose, and still Brother Haluin knelt, his crutches laid beside him.

Cadfael was the first to rise. It could not be long now to Prime, and it might be an inconvenient distraction to new young sisters to have two men in evidence at their morning service, even two monks of the same order. He crossed to the south door, and stood there looking out into the garth, waiting until Haluin should need his help to rise.

There was one of the sisters standing beside the stone bowl in the centre, very slender and erect and composed, feeding the birds. She crumbled bread on the broad rim of the bowl, and held fragments of it out on her open palm, and the flurry and vibration of hovering wings span fearlessly about her. The black habit became her slenderness, and her bearing had a youthful grace that stabbed piercingly into Cadfael's memory. The poise of the head on its long neck and straight shoulders, the narrow waist and elegant, long hand offering alms to the birds, these he had surely seen before, in another place, by another and deceptive light. Now she stood in open air, with the soft morning light upon her, and he could not believe that he was mistaken.

Helisende was here at Farewell, Helisende in a nun's habit. The bride had fled her unbearable dilemma to take the veil rather than marry anyone but her unfortunate lover Roscelin. True, she could not have taken any vows as yet, but the sisters might well see fit, in her stressful circumstances, to give her the instant protection of the habit, even before she entered on her novitiate.

She had quick hearing, or perhaps she had been expecting and listening for a light footstep in the western range of the cloister, where the sisters' dortoir lay. For plainly she caught the sound of someone approaching from that direction, and turned to meet the newcomer, smiling. The very movement, measured and tranquil, in itself cast doubt on the youth he had seen in her but a moment earlier, and showed him fully a face he had never seen before.

Not a young, unpractised girl, but a serene, worn, mature woman. The revelation in the hall at Vivers came about full circle, from illusion to reality, from the girl to the woman, as then it had spun headily backwards from the woman to the girl. Not Helisende, not even very like Helisende, but for the tall white ivory brow, and the sweet and plaintive oval shape of the face, and the wide-set, candid, gallant and vulnerable eyes. In figure and bearing, yes, the very same. If she had turned her back again, she would again have become the image of her daughter.

For who else could this be but the widowed mother who had taken the veil at Polesworth rather than be harried into a second marriage? Who else but Sister Benedicta, sent here to the bishop's new foundation to help to establish a secure tradition and a blessed example for the fledgling nuns of Farewell? Sister Benedicta who could charm flowers to grow and birds to come to her hand? Helisende must have known of her move, if the rest of the household at Vivers had not. Helisende had known where to look for refuge in her need. Where should she go but to her mother?

He had been concentrating so intensely upon the woman in the garth that he had heard nothing from within the church, until he caught the tapping of crutches on the flagstones within the doorway, and swung about almost guiltily to return to his bounden duty. Haluin had somehow got to his feet unaided, and emerged now at Cadfael's side, gazing out with pleasure into the garth, where misty sunlight and moist shadow mingled.

His eyes fell upon the nun, and he halted abruptly,

swaying on his crutches. Cadfael saw the dark eyes fix and widen, their arrested stare burning hollowly into the glowing stillness of vision or trance, and the sensitive lips move almost soundlessly, forming the slow syllables of a name. Almost soundlessly, but not quite, for Cadfael heard it.

In wonder and joy and pain, and all in extremes, as one driven and wracked by religious ecstasy: 'Bertrade!' whispered Brother Haluin.

Chapter Eleven

HERE WAS no mistaking the name, and no questioning the absolute certainty with which it was uttered. If Cadfael clung to sane, sensible disbelief for one moment, he discarded it the next, and it was swept away once for all in a great flood of enlightenment. In Haluin there was no doubt or question at all. He knew what he saw, he gave it its true, its unforgotten name, and stood lost in wonder, trembling with the intensity of his knowledge. Bertrade!

The first glimpse of her daughter had struck him to the heart, the dimly-seen copy outlined against the light was so true to the original. But as soon as Helisende had stepped forward into the torchlight the likeness had faded, the vision dissolved. This was a girl he did not know. Now she came again, and turned towards him the remembered and lamented face, and there was no more questioning.

So she had not died. Cadfael grappled silently with enlightenment. The tomb Haluin had sought was an illusion. She had not died of the draught that robbed her of her child, she had survived that peril and grief, to be married off to an elderly husband, vassal and friend to her mother's family, and to bear him a daughter the image of herself in

165

build and bearing. And she had done her best to be a faithful wife and mother as long as her old lord lived, but after his death she had turned her back on the world and followed her first lover into the cloister, choosing the same order, taking to herself the name of the founder, binding herself once for all to the same discipline into which Haluin had been driven.

Then why, argued a persistent imp in Cadfael's mind, why did you – *you*, not Haluin! – find in the face of the girl at Vivers something inexplicably familiar? Who was it hiding from you deep in the caverns of memory, refusing to be recognised? You had never seen the girl before, never in life set eyes on this mother of hers. Whoever looked out at you from Helisende's eyes, and then drew down a veil between, it was not Bertrade de Clary.

All this came seething through his mind in the instant of revelation, the brief moment before Helisende herself emerged from the shadows of the west range and came out into the garth to join her mother. She had not donned the habit, she wore the same gown she had worn the previous evening at her brother's table. She was pale and grave, but had the calm of the cloister about her, safe here from any compulsion, with time for thought and for taking counsel.

The two women met, the hems of their skirts tracing two darker paths in the silver-green of the moist grass. They turned back together at leisure towards the doorway from which Helisende had come, to go in and join the rest of the sisterhood for Prime. They were going away, they would vanish, and nothing be answered, nothing resolved, nothing made plain! And still Haluin hung swaying on his crutches, stricken motionless and mute. He would lose her again, she was all but lost already. The two women had almost reached the west walk, the cords of deprivation were drawn out to breaking point.

'Bertrade!' cried Haluin, in a great shout of terror and despair.

That cry reached them, echoing startlingly from every wall, and brought them about to stare in alarm and astonishment towards the door of the church. Haluin tore himself out of his daze with a great heave, and went hurtling forward recklessly into the garth, his crutches goring the soft turf.

At sight of an unknown man lurching towards them the women had instinctively recoiled, but seeing at second glance his habit, and how sadly he was crippled, in pure compassion they halted their flight to permit his approach, and even came a few impulsive steps to meet him. For a moment there was no more in it than that, pity for a lame man. Then abruptly everything changed.

He had been in too much haste to reach them, he stumbled, and swayed out of balance for a moment, on the edge of a fall, and the girl, quick to sympathy, sprang forward to support him in her arms. His weight falling into her embrace swung them both about, to steady and recover almost cheek to cheek, and Cadfael saw the two faces for a long moment side by side, startled, bright, dazzled into wonder.

So now at last he had his answer. Now he knew everything there was to be known, everything except what fury of bitterness could drive one human creature to do so base and cruel a thing to another. And even that answer would not be far to seek.

It was at that moment of total enlightenment that Bertrade de Clary, staring earnestly into the stranger's face, knew him for no stranger, and called him by his name:

'Haluin!'

There was nothing more, not then, only the meeting of eyes and the mutual recognition, and the understanding, on either part, of past wrongs and agonies never before fully understood, bitter and terrible for a moment, then erased by

a great flood of gratitude and joy. For in the moment when
the three of them hung mute and still, staring at one another,
they all heard the little bell for Prime ringing in the dortoir,
and knew that the sisters would be filing down the night
stairs to walk in procession into the church.

So there was nothing more, not then. The women drew
back, with lingering glances still wide with wonder, and
turned to answer the summons and join their sisters. And
Cadfael went forward from the porch to take Brother
Haluin by the arm, and lead him gently, like a sleep-walking
child, back to the guest-hall.

'She is not dead,' said Haluin, rigidly erect on the edge of
his bed. Over and over, recording the miracle in a repetition
nearer incantation than prayer: 'She is not dead! It was
false, false, false! She did not die!'

Cadfael said never a word. It was not yet time to speak of
all that lay behind this revelation. For the moment Haluin's
shocked mind looked no further than the fact, the joy that
she should be alive and well and in safe haven whom he had
lamented so long as dead, and dead by his grievous fault,
the bewilderment and hurt that he should have been left so
long mourning her.

'I must speak with her,' said Haluin. 'I cannot go without
having speech with her.'

'You shall not,' Cadfael assured him.

It was inevitable now, all must come out. They had met,
they had beheld each other, no one now could undo that,
the sealed coffer was sprung open, the secrets were
tumbling out of it, no one now could close the lid upon
them ever again.

'We cannot leave today,' said Haluin.

'We shall not. Wait here in patience,' said Cadfael. 'I am
going to seek an audience with the lady abbess.'

*　　*　　*

The abbess of Farewell, brought by Bishop de Clinton from Coventry to direct his new foundation, was a dumpy round loaf of a woman, perhaps in her middle forties, with a plump russet face and shrewd brown eyes that weighed and measured in a glance, and were confident of their judgement. She sat uncompromisingly erect on an uncushioned bench in a small and Spartan parlour, and closed the book on the desk before her as Cadfael came in.

'You're very welcome, Brother, to whatever service our house can offer you. Ursula tells me you are from the abbey of Saint Peter and Saint Paul, at Shrewsbury. I intended to invite you and your companion to join me for dinner, and I cordially extend that invitation now. But I hear you have asked for this interview, forestalling any move of mine. I take it there is a reason. Sit down, Brother, and tell me what more you have to ask of me.'

Cadfael sat down with her, debating in his mind how much he might tell, or how little. She was a woman quite capable of filling in gaps for herself, but also, he judged, a woman of scrupulous discretion, who would keep to herself whatever she read between the lines.

'I come, Reverend Mother, to ask you to countenance a meeting, in private, between my brother Haluin and Sister Benedicta.'

He saw her brows raised, but the small bright eyes beneath them remained unperturbed and sharp with intelligence.

'In youth,' he said, 'they were well acquainted. He was in her mother's service, and being so close in the one house, and of an age, boy and girl together, they fell into loving. But Haluin's suit was not at all to her mother's mind, and she took pains to separate them. Haluin was dismissed from her service, and forbidden all ado with the girl, who was persuaded into a marriage more pleasing to her family. No doubt you know her history since then. Haluin entered our house, admittedly for a wrong reason. It is not good to turn

169

to the spiritual life out of despair, but many have done it, as you and I know, and lived to become faithful and honourable ornaments to their houses. So has Haluin. So, I make no doubt, has Bertrade de Clary.'

He caught the glint of her eyes at hearing that name. There was not much she did not know about her flock, but if she knew more than he had said of this woman she showed no sign and made no comment, accepting all as he had told it.

'It seems to me,' she said, 'that the story you tell me bids fair to be repeated in another generation. The circumstances are not quite the same, but the end well could be. It's as well we should consider in time how to deal with it.'

'I have that in mind,' said Cadfael. 'And how have you dealt with it thus far? Since the girl came running to you by night? For the whole household of Vivers is out by now for the second day, scouring the roads for her.'

'I think not,' said the abbess. 'For I sent yesterday to let her brother know that she is here and safe, and prays him to be left in peace here for a while for thought and prayer. I think he will respect her wish, in the circumstances.'

'Circumstances which she has told you,' said Cadfael with conviction, 'in full. So far, that is, as she knows them.'

'She has.'

'Then you know of a woman's death, and of the marriage arranged for Helisende. And the reason for that marriage, you know that, too?'

'I know she is too close kin to the young man she would liefer have. Yes, she has told me. More, I fancy, than she tells her confessor. You need not fear for Helisende, as long as she remains here she is safe from all harassment, and has the company and comfort of her mother.'

'She could not be in a better place,' said Cadfael fervently. 'Then, as to these two who most concern us now – I

170

must tell you that Haluin was told that Bertrade was dead, and has believed her so all these years, and moreover, taken her death to himself as blame. This morning by God's grace he has seen her before him alive and well. They have exchanged no words but their names. But I think it would be well that they should, if you so grant. They will serve better in their separate vocations if they have peace of mind. Also they have a right to know, each one, that the other is whole, blessed and content.'

'And you think,' said the abbess with deliberation, 'that they *will* be blessed and content? After as before?'

'More and better than before,' he said with certainty. 'I can speak for the man, if you know as much of the woman. And if they part thus without a word, they will be tormented to the end of their days.'

'I would as soon not be answerable to God for that,' said the abbess, with a brief, bleak smile. 'Well, they shall have their hour and make their peace. It can do no harm, and may do much good. Do you purpose to remain here some days longer?'

'This one day at least,' said Cadfael. 'For I have one more prayer to make to you. Brother Haluin I leave to you. But there is a thing I must do, before we set off for home. Not here! Will you let me borrow a horse from your stable?'

She sat studying him for a long moment, and it seemed that she was guardedly satisfied with what she saw, for at length she said: 'On one condition.'

'And that is?'

'That when time serves, and all harm is spent, you will tell me the other half of the story.'

Brother Cadfael led out his borrowed horse into the stable-yard, and mounted without haste. The bishop had seen fit to provide stabling adequate for his own visitations, and two stout cobs for remounts should any of his envoys travel this way and make use of the abbey's hospitality. Having been given a free hand, Cadfael had naturally chosen the more likely looking of the two, and the younger, a lively, solid bay. It was no very long ride he had in mind, but he might as well get out of it what pleasure he could along the way. There would be little pleasure at the end of it.

The sun was already high when he rode out at the gate, a pale sun growing brighter and clearer as the air of the day warmed into palpable spring. The fatal snow at Vivers would be the last snow of the winter, appropriately completing Haluin's pilgrimage, as the first snow had begun it.

The filigree green gauze of buds along the branches of bush and tree had burst into the tender plumage of young leaves. The moist grass shimmered, and gave off a faint, fragrant steam as the sun reached it. So much beauty, and behind him as he rode lay a great mercy, a just deliverance, and the renewal of hope. And before him a solitary soul to be saved or lost.

He did not take the road to Vivers. It was not there he had urgent business, though he might well return that way. Once he halted to look back, and the long line of the abbey fence had disappeared in the folds of land, and the hamlet with it. Haluin would be waiting and wondering, groping his way through a confused dream, beset with questions to which he could have no answer, torn between belief and disbelief, fearful joy and recollected anguish, until the abbess should send to summon him to the meeting which would make all things plain at last.

Cadfael rode on slowly until he should encounter someone from whom he could ask directions. A woman leading sheep and lambs out to pasture at the edge of the village stopped willingly to point him to the most direct road. He need not go near Vivers, and that was well, for he had no wish to meet Cenred or his men as yet. He had nothing at this moment to tell them, and indeed it was not he who must tell what finally had to be told.

Once on the track his informant had indicated, he rode fast and purposefully, until he dismounted at the gate of the manor of Elford.

It was the young portress who tapped at the door and entered Brother Haluin's haunted solitude, later in the morning, when the sun had shed its veil, and the grass of the garth was drying. He looked round as she came in, expecting Cadfael, and gazed at her with eyes still wide and blank with wonder.

'I am sent by the lady abbess,' said the girl, with solicitous gentleness, since it seemed he might be almost beyond understanding, 'to bid you to her parlour. If you will come with me, I'll show you the way.'

Obediently he reached for his crutches. 'Brother Cadfael went forth and has not returned,' he said slowly, looking about him like a man awaking from sleep. 'Is this bidding to him also? Should I not wait for him?'

'There is no need,' she said. 'Brother Cadfael has already spoken with Mother Patrice, and has an errand he says he must do now. You should wait for his return here, and be easy. Will you come?'

Haluin thrust himself to his feet and went with her, across the rear court to the abbess's lodging, confiding like a child though half his mind was still absent. The little portress tempered her flying steps to his laboured gait, bringing him with considerate gentleness to the door of the parlour, and turning upon him on the threshold a bright, encouraging smile.

'Go in, you are expected.'

She held the door open for him, since he had need of both hands for his crutches. He limped across the threshold into the wood-scented, dimly lit room, and halted just within to make his reverence to the Mother Superior, only to stand motionless and quivering as his eyes adjusted to the subdued light. For the woman who stood waiting for him, braced and still and wonderfully smiling in the centre of the room, her hands extended instinctively to aid his approach, was not the abbess, but Bertrade de Clary.

Chapter Twelve

HE GROOM who came unhurriedly across the courtyard to greet the visitor and enquire his business was neither Lothair nor Luc, but a lanky lad not yet twenty, with a shock of dark hair. At his back the courtyard seemed emptied of its usual lively activity, only a few maids and manservants going back and forth about their work in a casual fashion, as if all constraints were slackened. By the look of things, the master of the house and most of his men were still out and about on the hunt for any word that might lead to the murderer of Edgytha.

'If you're wanting the lord Audemar,' said the boy at once, 'you're out of luck. He's still away to Vivers about this woman who was killed a couple of nights back. But his steward's here, if you want lodging you'd best see him.'

'I thank you,' said Cadfael, surrendering his bridle, 'but it's not the lord Audemar I've come to see. My errand is to his mother. I know where her dower apartments are. If you'll see to the horse I'll go myself and ask her woman to enquire if the lady will be good enough to see me.'

'As you please, then. You were here afore,' said the lad, narrowing his eyes curiously at this vaguely familiar visitor.

'Only a few days back, with another black monk, one that went on crutches and very lame.'

'True,' said Cadfael. 'And I had speech with the lady then, and she will not have forgotten either me or that lame brother. If she refuses me a hearing now, I will let her be – but I think she will not refuse.'

'Try for yourself, then,' agreed the groom indifferently. 'She's still here with her maid, and I know she's within. She keeps within, these last days.'

'She had two grooms with her,' said Cadfael, 'father and son. We were acquainted, when we stayed here, they had come from Shropshire with her. I'd willingly pass the time of day with them, afterwards, if they're not away to Vivers with the lord Audemar's people.'

'Oh, them! No, they're her fellows, none of his. But they're not here, neither. They went off yesterday on some errand of hers, very early. Where? How should I know where? Back to Hales, likely. That's where the old dame keeps, most of her time.'

I wonder, thought Cadfael, as he turned towards Adelais's dwelling in the corner of the enclave wall, and the groom led the cob away to the stable, truly I wonder how it would suit Adelais de Clary to know that her son's grooms speak of her as 'the old dame'. Doubtless to that raw boy she seemed ancient as the hills, but resolutely she cherished and conserved what had once been great beauty, and from that excellence nothing and no one must be allowed to detract. Not for nothing did she choose for her intimate maid someone plain and pockmarked, surrounding herself with dull and ordinary faces that caused her own lustre to glow more brightly.

At the door of Adelais's hall he asked for audience, and the woman Gerta came out to him haughtily, protective of her mistress's privacy and assertive of her own office. He had sent in no name, and at sight of him she checked, none too pleased to see one of the Benedictines from Shrewsbury back again so soon, and so unaccountably.

'My lady is not disposed to see visitors. What's your business, that you need trouble her with it? If you need lodging and food, my lord Audemar's steward will take care of it.'

'My business,' said Cadfael, 'is with the lady Adelais only, and concerns no one beside. Tell her that Brother Cadfael is here again, and that he comes from the abbey of Farewell, and asks to have some talk with her. That she shuns visitors I believe. But I think she will not refuse me.'

She was not so bold that she dared take it upon herself to deny him, though she went with a toss of her head and a disdainful glance, and would have been glad to bring back a dismissive answer. It was plain by the sour look on her face when she emerged from the solar that she was denied that pleasure.

'My lady bids you in,' she said coldly, and opened the door wide for him to pass by her and enter the chamber. And no doubt she hoped to linger and be privy to whatever passed, but favour did not extend so far.

'Leave us,' said the voice of Adelais de Clary, from deep shadow under a shuttered window. 'And close the door between.'

She had no seemly woman's occupation for her hands this time, no pretence at embroidering or spinning, she merely sat in her great chair in semi-darkness, motionless, her hands spread along the arms and gripping the carved lion-heads in which they terminated. She did not move as Cadfael came in, she was neither surprised nor disturbed. Her deep eyes burned upon him without wonder, and he thought without regret. It was almost as though she had been waiting for him.

'Where have you left Haluin?' she asked.

'At the abbey of Farewell,' said Cadfael.

She was silent for a moment, brooding upon him with a still face and glowing eyes, with an intensity he felt as a vibration upon the air, before ever his eyes had grown accustomed to the dim light, and watched her lineaments grow gradually out of darkness, the chosen darkness in which she had incarcerated herself. Then she said with harsh deliberation: 'I shall never see him again.'

'No, you will never see him again. When this is done, we are going home.'

'But you,' she said, 'yes, I have had it in mind all this time that you would be back. Sooner or later, you would be back. As well, perhaps! Things have gone far beyond my reckoning now. Well, say what you have come to say. I would as lief be silent.'

'That you cannot do,' said Cadfael. 'It is your story.'

'Then be my chronicler. Tell it! Remind me! Let me hear how it will sound in my confessor's ears, if any priest takes my confession ever again.' She stretched out one long hand suddenly, waving him imperiously to a seat, but he remained standing where he could see her most clearly, and she made no move to evade his eyes, and no concessions to the fixity of his regard. Her beautiful, proud face was composed and mute, admitting nothing, denying nothing. Only the burning of her dark eyes in their deep settings was eloquent, and even that in a language he could not quite translate.

'You know all too well what you did, all those years ago,' said Cadfael. 'You executed a fearful punishment upon Haluin for daring to love your daughter and getting her with child. You pursued him even into the cloister where your enmity had driven him – all too soon, but the young are quick to despair. You forced him to provide you with the means of abortion, and you sent him word, afterwards, that it had killed both mother and child. That awful guilt you have visited upon him all these years, to be his torment lifelong. Did you speak?'

'No,' she said. 'Go on! You have barely begun.'

'True, I have barely begun. That draught of hyssop and fleur de luce that you got from him – it never was used. Its purpose was only to poison him, it did no harm to any other. What did you do with it? Pour it away into the ground? No, long before ever you demanded the herbs from him, as soon as you had driven him out of your house, I daresay, you had hustled Bertrade away here to Elford, and married her to Edric Vivers. It must have been so, certainly it was done in time to give her child, when it was born, a credible if unlikely father. No doubt the old man prided himself on still being potent enough to get a child. Why should anyone question the birth-date, since you had acted so quickly?'

She had not stirred or flinched, her eyes never left his face, admitting nothing, denying nothing.

'Were you never afraid,' he asked, 'that someone, somehow, should let fall within reach even of the cloister that Bertrade de Clary was wife to Edric Vivers, and not safely in her grave? That she had borne her old husband a daughter? It needed only a chance traveller with a gossiping tongue.'

'There was no such risk,' she said simply. 'What contact was there ever between Shrewsbury and Hales? None, until he suffered his fall and conceived his pilgrimage. Much less likely there should ever be dealings with manors in another shire. There was no such risk.'

'Well, let us continue. Living you took her away and gave her to a husband. Living the child was born. So much mercy at least you had on the girl – why none for him? Why such bitter and vindictive hate, that you should conceive so terrible a revenge? Not for your daughter's wrongs, no! Why should he not have been considered a suitable match for her in the first place? He came of good family, he was heir to a

179

fine manor, if he had not taken the cowl. What was it you held so much against him? You were a beautiful woman, accustomed to admiration and homage. Your lord was in Palestine. And I well remember Haluin as he first came to me, eighteen years old, not yet tonsured. I saw him as you had been seeing him for some few years in your celibate solitude – he was comely . . .'

He let it rest there, for her long, resolute lips had parted on deliberate affirmation at last. She had listened to him unwaveringly, making no effort to halt him, and no complaint. Now she responded.

'Too comely!' she said. 'I was not used to being denied, I did not even know how to sue. And he was too innocent to read me aright. How such children offend without offence! So if I could not have him,' she said starkly, 'she should not. No woman ever should, but not she of all women.'

It was said, she let it stand, adding nothing in extenuation, and having said it, she sat contemplating it, seeing again as in another woman what she could now no longer feel with the same intensity, the longing and the anger.

'There is more,' said Cadfael, 'much more. There is the matter of your woman Edgytha. Edgytha was the one trusted confidante you needed, the one who knew the truth. It was she who was sent to Vivers with Bertrade. Utterly loyal and devoted to you, she kept your secret and abetted your revenge all these years. And you trusted in her to keep it for ever. So all was well for you, until Roscelin and Helisende grew up, and came to love each other no longer as playmates, but as man and woman. Knowing but forgetting that the world would hold such a love as poisoned, guilty, forbidden by the church. When the secret became a barrier between them, where no barrier need have been, when Roscelin was banished to Elford, and marriage with de Perronet threatened a final separation, then Edgytha could bear it no longer. She came running here in the night – not to Roscelin, but to you! To beg you to tell the truth at last, or to give her leave to tell it for you.'

'I have wondered,' said Adelais, 'how she knew that I was here within her reach.'

'She knew because I told her. All unwitting I sent her out that night to plead with you to lift the shadow from two innocent children. By merest chance it was mentioned that here in Elford we had spoken with you. *I* sent her running to you and to her death, as it was Haluin who caused you to come here, in haste to ward him off from any dangerous discovery. We have been the instruments of your undoing, who never wished you anything but well. Now you had better consider what is left to you that can be saved.'

'Go on!' she said harshly. 'You have not finished yet.'

'No, not yet. So Edgytha came to plead with you to do right. And you refused her! You sent her running back to Vivers in despair. And what befell her on the way you know.'

She did not deny it. Her face was bleak and set, but her eyes never wavered.

'Would she have come out with the truth, even against your prohibition? Neither you nor I will ever know the answer to that. But someone equally loyal to you overheard enough to understand the threat to you if she did. Someone feared her, followed and silenced her. Oh, not you! You had other tools to use. But did you speak a word in their ears?'

'No!' said Adelais. 'That I never did! Unless my face spoke for me. And if it did, it lied. I never would have harmed her.'

'I believe you. But which of them was it followed her? Father and son alike, they would die for you without question, and without question one of them has killed for you. And they are gone from here. Back to Hales? No, I doubt that, it is not far enough. How distant is your son's remotest manor?'

'You will not find them,' said Adelais with certainty. 'As for which of them did the thing I might have prevented, I do not know, I want never to know. I stopped their mouths when they would have spoken. To what end? That guilt, like all the rest, is mine alone, I will not cede any scruple of it. Yes, I sent them away. They will not pay my debts for me. Burying Edgytha with reverence is poor atonement. Confession, penance, even absolution cannot restore a life.'

'There is one amend that can still be made,' said Cadfael. 'Moreover, I think a price has been exacted from you, no less than from Haluin, all these years. Do not forget that I saw your face when he presented his ruined body before you. I heard your voice as you cried out on him: "What have they done to you?" All that you did to him you did also to yourself, and once done, it could not be undone. Now you may be free of it, if you choose to deliver yourself.'

'Go on!' said Adelais, though she knew well enough what was to come. He recognised it by the composure with which she had borne herself throughout. Surely she had been waiting here in her half-lit room for the finger of God to point.

'Helisende is not Edric's daughter, but Haluin's. There is not a drop of Vivers blood in her veins. There is nothing to stand in the way if she wishes to marry Roscelin. Whether those two would do well to marry, who knows? But at least the shadow of incestuous affection can and must be lifted from them. The truth must out, since it is out already at Farewell. Haluin and Bertrade are there together, making their peace, making each the other's peace, and Helisende their child is with them, and the truth is already out of its grave.'

She knew, she had known ever since the old woman's death, that it must come to that at last, and if she had deliberately averted her eyes and refused to acknowledge it, she could no longer do so. Nor was she the woman to delegate a hard thing to others, once her mind was made up, nor to do things by halves, whether for good or ill.

He would not prompt her. He drew back from her to leave her space and time, and stood apart, watching her disciplined stillness, and measuring in his mind the bitter toll of eighteen years of silence, of pitilessly contained hate and love. The first words he had heard from her now, even at this extreme, had been of Haluin, and still he heard the vibration of pain in her voice as she cried aloud: 'What have they done to you?'

Adelais got up abruptly from her chair and crossed with long, fierce steps to the window, to fling back the shutter and let in air and light and cold. She stood for a while looking out at the quiet court, and the pale sky dappled with little clouds, and the green gauze veiling the branches of the trees beyond the enclave wall. When she turned to him again he saw her face in full, clear light, and saw as in a dual vision both her imperishable beauty and the dust time had cast upon it, the taut lines of her long throat fallen slack, the grey of ashes in her coiled black hair, the lines that had gathered about mouth and eyes, the net of fine veins marring cheeks which had once been smooth ivory. And she was strong, she would not lightly relinquish her hold of the world and go gently out of it. She would live long, and rage against the relentless assault of old age until death at once defeated and released her. By her very nature Adelais's penance was assured.

'No!' she said, with abrupt, imperious authority, as though he had advanced some suggestion with which she was in absolute disagreement. 'No, I want no advocate, there shall no man rid me of any part of what is mine. What now needs to be told, *I* will tell. No other! Whether it ever would have been told, if you had never come near me – you with your hand for ever at Haluin's elbow, and your temperate eyes that I could never read – do I know? Do you? That is of no account now. What is left to be done, *I* will do.'

'Command me to go,' said Cadfael, 'and I will go. You do not need me.'

'Not as advocate, no. As witness, perhaps! Why should you be cheated of the ending? Yes!' she said, glittering. 'You shall ride with me, and see it ended. I owe you a fulfilment as I owe God a death.'

He rode with her, as she had decreed. Why not? He had to return to Farewell, and by way of Vivers was as good a road as any. And once she had resolved upon action there could be no delay and no denial.

She rode astride, booted and spurred like a man, she who in the common progressions of her recent years had been content to go decorously pillion behind a groom, as was fitting for a dame of her age and dignity. She rode with the lordly confidence of a man, erect and easy in the saddle, her bridle hand held low. And she rode fast but steadily, advancing upon her losses as vigorously as upon her gains.

Cadfael, riding at her side, could not but wonder whether she still felt tempted to hold back some part of the truth, to cover herself from the last betrayal. But the smouldering calm of her face spoke against it. There would be no evasion, no appeal, no excuse. What she had done she had done, and would as starkly declare. And if she repented it, only God would ever know.

Chapter Thirteen

HEY RODE in at the gate of Vivers an hour
after noon. The gate stood open, and the turmoil
within had subsided, there was no more than the
normal to-and-froing in the court. Evidently the
abbess's messenger had been received and believed, and
whether gladly or reluctantly, Cenred had fallen in with
Helisende's wish to be left alone for a while in her sanctuary.
With one search abandoned, Audemar's men would be free
to pursue a murderer. One they would never find! In the
night and the snow, who could have been abroad to witness
that knife-stroke in the woods, and put a name or a face to
the slayer? Even if there had been a witness, who in these
parts, apart from Audemar's own household, would recog-
nise a groom from distant Hales?

Cenred's steward was crossing the court when Adelais
reined in, and he came in haste, recognising the mother of
his lord's overlord, to help her down, but she was out of the
saddle before he could reach her. She let down her kilted
skirts, and looked about her for any of her son's people.
Cadfael had seen for himself that the hunters had not
returned to Elford, nor were they in evidence here. For a
moment she frowned, impatient at the prospect of having to

wait and contain still all that she had to say. Once resolved, it displeased her to be baulked. She looked beyond the steward's deep reverence towards the hall.

'Is your lord within?'

'He is, madam. Will you be pleased to enter?'

'And my son?'

'He, too, my lady. He came back only some minutes since, his men are still out with ours, questioning in every house for miles around.'

'Waste of time!' she said, rather to herself than to him, and shut her lips grimly on the reason. 'Well, so much the better! They are both here. No, you need not tell them I have come. That I'll do for myself. As for Brother Cadfael, this time he comes in attendance on me, not as a guest.'

Doubtful if the steward had even cast a glance at the second rider until this moment, but he did so now, speculating, Cadfael supposed, what had brought one Benedictine visitor back so soon, and in particular without his companion. But there was no time for enquiry. Adelais had set off vigorously towards the steps that led up to the hall, and Cadfael followed dutifully, as if he were indeed her domestic chaplain, leaving the steward staring after them in doubt and wonder.

In the hall the midday meal was past, and the servants busy clearing away the dishes and stacking the tables aside. Adelais walked through them without a word or a glance, straight to the curtained door of the inner chamber. A murmur of voices, dulled by the hangings, came from within, Cenred's deep tones distinguishable beneath the lighter, younger voice of Jean de Perronet. The suitor had not withdrawn, but intended to wait out his time doggedly if not patiently. Just as well, Cadfael reflected. He had a right to know how formidable an obstacle was now placed in his way. Fair is fair. De Perronet had done nothing dishonourable, fair dealing was his due.

Adelais swept the curtain aside and flung open the door. They were all there, in muted conference over a situation which left them frustrated and helpless, trapped in inaction, since even the gesture of sending out men to try and trace Edgytha's murderer was by this time foredoomed to be fruitless. Had any man in the region known anything, it would have been told already. And if Audemar ever thought to number over his mother's household servants, and level a suspicious finger at the missing, she would stand immovably between him and them. Wherever Lothair and Luc might now be, however confounded and chastened by her revulsion from what they had mistakenly done for her, she would not let the price be charged against them which she held to be her debt.

At the sound of the door opening they had all turned their heads sharply to see who came in, for her entrance was too abrupt and confident by far for any of the servants. Her gaze swept round the circle of surprised faces, Audemar and Cenred at the table with wine before them, Emma apart at her embroidery frame, but paying no attention to the work, rather waiting with strung nerves for events to unfold in some more comfortable form, and life to return to its level course. And the stranger – Cadfael saw that Adelais could never before have set eyes on Jean de Perronet. On him her glance halted, considering and identifying the bridegroom. Very faintly and briefly her long lips contorted in a dour smile, before her eyes passed to Roscelin.

The boy sat withdrawn into a corner where he could hold all the assembled company in his eye, as if he contemplated imminent battle, and sat prepared and armed, stiff and erect on the bench against the tapestried wall, head reared and lips tightly set. He had accepted, it seemed, however much against his will, Helisende's wish to be left in peace at Farewell, but he had not forgiven any of these conspirators who had planned to match her in secret, and cheat him of even the perverse hope he had to sustain him. His grievance against his parents extended by contagion to de Perronet, even to Audemar de Clary, to whose house he had been banished to remove the obstacle to their plans. How could he be sure Audemar had not been a party to more than that banishment? A face by nature open, good-humoured and bright now stared upon them all closed, suspicious and inimical. Adelais looked at him longer than at any. Another youth too comely for his own good, attracting unfortunate love as the flower draws the bee.

The moment of blank surprise was over. Cenred was on his feet in hospitable haste, advancing with hand outstretched to take the visitor by the hand, and lead her to a seat at the table.

'Madam, welcome to my house! You do me honour!'

And Audemar, less pleased, half frowning: 'Madam, what brings you here? And unattended!' It suited him better that a mother of so formidable a character should exile herself to the distant manor of Hales, and keep her own court there. Seeing them thus face to face, Cadfael found a strong likeness between the two. Doubtless there was affection between them, but once the son was grown it would be hard for these two to live together in one household. 'There was no need,' said Audemar, 'for you to ride over here, there is nothing you can do that is not already being done.'

Adelais had let Cenred's attentive hand persuade her into the centre of the room, but there she resisted further movement and stood to be seen clearly and alone, with an authoritative gesture freeing her hand.

'Yes,' she said, 'there is need,' and again cast a long glance round all the watching faces. 'And I am not unattended. Brother Cadfael is my escort. He comes from the abbey of Farewell, and will be returning there when he leaves us.' She looked from one young man to the other, from the favoured bridegroom to the frustrated lover, both of them eyeing her warily, conscious of impending revelations, but unable to hazard at what might be coming.

'I am glad,' said Adelais, 'to find you all assembled thus. I have that to say that I will say only once.'

It could never have been a problem for her, thought Cadfael, watching, to hold the attention of everyone about her, wherever she went. In every room she entered she was at once the focal point, the dominant in every company. Now they were silent every one, waiting on her word.

'As I have heard, Cenred,' she said, 'you intended, two days ago, to marry your sister – your half-sister I should say – to this young gentleman. For reason enough, the church and the world would agree, seeing she had become all too dear to your son Roscelin, and he to her, and a marriage that would take her far away removed also the shadow of such an unholy attachment from your house and from your heir. Pardon me if I use too plain words, it's late for any others. No blame to you, knowing only what you knew.'

'What more was there to know?' said Cenred, bewildered.

'Plain words will do very well. They are close blood-kin, as you know well! Would not you have taken the same measure to ward off such an evil from your grandchild, as I intended from my sister? She is as close a charge to me as my own son, and as dear. She is your grandchild. I well remember my father's second marriage. I recall the day you brought the bride here, and my father's pride in the child she bore him. Since he is long gone, I owe Helisende a father's care no less than a brother's. Certainly I sought to protect both her and my son. I still desire the same. This is but a check on the way. Messire de Perronet has not withdrawn his suit, nor I my sanction.'

Audemar had risen from his place, and stood eyeing his mother with close-drawn brows and an unrevealing face. 'What more is there to know?' he said levelly, and for all his voice was equable and low there was doubt and displeasure in it, and a woman of less implacable will might have found it menacing. She stared back at him eye to eye, and was unmoved.

'This! That you trouble needless. There is no barrier, Cenred, between your son and Helisende but the barrier you have conjured up. There is no peril of incest if they were wedded and bedded this very night. Helisende is not your sister, Cenred, she is not your father's daughter. There is no drop of Vivers blood in her veins.'

'But this is foolishness!' protested Cenred, shaking his head over so incredible a claim. 'All this household has known the child from birth. What you say is impossible. Why bring forth such a story, when all my people can bear witness she was born to my father's lawful wife, in their marriage bed, here in my house.'

And conceived in mine,' said Adelais. 'I can't wonder if none of you thought to count the days, I had lost no time. My daughter was already with child when I brought her here to her marriage.'

Then they were all on their feet, all but Emma, shrinking appalled behind her embroidery frame, shaken by the out-cries of anger and disbelief that clashed about her like contrary winds. Cenred was stricken breathless, but de Perronet was clamouring that this was false, and the lady out of her wits, and Roscelin had sprung to confront him, glittering, half incoherent, swinging about from his rival to Adelais, pleading, demanding, that what she said be truth. Until Audemar pounded the table thunderously with his fist, and raised an imperious voice over all to demand silence. And throughout, Adelais stood erect and unmoving as stone, and let the outcries whirl about her unacknowledged.

And then there was silence, no more exclaiming, not a sound, hardly a breath, while they stared upon her intently

190

and long, as if the truth or falsity of what she said might be read in her face if a man held still and unblinking long enough.

'Do you fully know, madam, what you are saying?' asked Audemar, his voice now measured and low.

'Excellently well, my son! I know what I am saying, I know it is truth. I know what I have done, I know it was foully done. It needs none of you to say it, *I* say it. But I did it, and neither you nor I can undo it. Yes, I deceived the lord Edric, yes, I compelled my daughter, yes, I planted a bastard child in this house. Or, if you choose, I took measures to protect my daughter's good name and estate and ensure her honourable status, as Cenred wills to do for a sister. Did Edric ever regret his bargain? I think not. Did he get joy out of his supposed child? Surely he did. All these years I have let well or ill alone, but now God has disposed otherwise, and I am not sorry.'

'If this is true,' said Cenred, drawing deep breath, 'Edgytha knew of it. She came here with Bertrade, if you are telling truth now, so late, then she must have known.'

'She did know,' said Adelais. 'And sorry the day I refused her when she begged me to tell the truth earlier, and sorrier still this day when she cannot stand here and bear me witness. But here is one who can. Brother Cadfael is come from the abbey of Farewell, where Helisende now is, and her mother is there with her. And by strange chance,' she said, 'so is her father. There is nowhere now to hide from the truth. I declare it in my own despite.'

'You have hidden from it long enough, madam, it seems,' said Audemar grimly.

'So I have, and make no virtue of revealing it now, when it is already out of its grave.'

There was a brief, profound silence before Cenred asked slowly: 'You say he is there now – her father? There at Farewell with them both?'

'From me,' she said, 'it can only be hearsay. Brother Cadfael will answer you.'

'I have seen them there, all three,' said Cadfael. 'It is truth.'

'Then who is he?' demanded Audemar. 'Who is her father?'

Adelais took up her story, never lowering her eyes. 'He was once a young clerk in my household, of good birth, only a year older than my daughter. He desired to be accepted as a suitor for her hand. I refused him. They – took measures to force my hand. No, perhaps I do them both wrong, what they did may not have been calculated, but done in desperation, for she was as lost in love as he. I dismissed him from my service, and brought her away here in haste, to a match the lord Edric had mooted a year or more earlier. And I lied, telling the lover that she was dead. Very blackly I lied to him, saying both Bertrade and her child had died, when we tried to rid her of her burden. He never knew until now that he had a daughter.'

'Then how comes it,' demanded Cenred, 'that he has found her out now, and in so unlikely a place? This whole wild story comes so strangely, thus out of nowhere, I cannot believe in it.'

'You had better come to terms with it,' she said, 'for neither you nor I can escape the truth or amend it. He has found her by the merciful dispensation of God. What more do you need?'

Cenred swung upon Cadfael in irritated appeal. 'Brother, as you have been my guest in this house, tell what you know of this matter. After so many years, is this indeed a true tale? And how came these three to meet again now, at the end of all?'

'It is a true tale,' said Cadfael. 'And truly they have met, by now they will have talked together. He has found them both because, believing his love dead, and having touched hands with his own death a few months ago, and been spared, he turned his thoughts to mortality, and determined at least, since he could never see her again in this world, to make a pilgrimage to her grave and pray for her peace in the next. And not finding her at Hales, where he supposed she must be, he came here, my lord, to your manor of Elford, where those of your line are buried. Now, on the way home again, by the grace of God we asked lodging last night at the abbey of Farewell. There the lady who was your sister is presently serving as instructress to the novices of the bishop's new foundation. And there Helisende fled for sanctuary from too painful stresses. So they are all under one roof at last.'

After a moment of silence Audemar said softly: '*We* asked lodging last night at the abbey of Farewell' – You have said almost enough, yet add one thing more – name him!'

'He entered the cloister, long ago. He is a brother with me in the abbey of Saint Peter and Saint Paul, at Shrewsbury. You have seen him, my lord, that same brother who came to Elford with me, on crutches every step of the way. Monk and priest, the same, my lord Cenred, whom you asked to marry Helisende to the man you had chosen for her. His name is Haluin.'

Now they had all begun dazedly to believe what they could not yet fully grasp in all its implications. With glazed glances they stared within at the slow realisation of what this must mean to them. To Roscelin, quivering and glowing like a newly lighted torch, the sudden dizzy lightness and liberty of guilt and grief lifted from him, the very air of the day intoxicating as wine, the world expanded into a vast brightness of hope and joy that dazzled his eyes and muted his tongue. To de Perronet, the stinging challenge of finding himself faced with a formidable rival where he had looked for no conflict, and the instinctive stiffening of his pride and determination to fight for the threatened prize with all his might. To Cenred the overturning of all his family memories, a father made to seem belittled, even senile, by his fond acceptance of such a deception, a sister abruptly withdrawn into a stranger, an interloper without rights in his house. To Emma, silent and fearful in her corner, the grief of an offence against her lord, and the loss of one she had looked upon almost as her own daughter.

'So she is no sister of mine,' said Cenred heavily, rather to himself than to any other, and as quickly repeated it with sudden anger to them all: 'She is no sister of mine!'

'None,' said Adelais. 'But until now she believed herself so. It is not her fault, never cast blame on her.'

'She is not kin to me. I owe her nothing, neither dowry nor lands. She has no claim on me.' He said it bitterly rather than vengefully, lamenting the abrupt severance of a strong affection.

'None. But she is kin to me,' said Adelais. 'Her mother's dower lands went to Polesworth when she took the veil, but Helisende is my granddaughter and my heiress. The lands I hold in my own right will go to her. She will not be penniless.' She looked at de Perronet as she spoke, and smiled, but wryly. No need to make the lovers' path too smooth by rendering the girl less profitable, and therefore less attractive in the rival's eyes.

'Madam, you mistake me,' said Cenred with muted fury. 'This house has been her home, she will still think of it as home. Where else is there for her? It is we here who are suddenly cut off, like lopped limbs. Her father and mother, both, are in the cloister, and what guidance, what care has she ever had from you? Kin to us or not, she belongs here at Vivers.'

'But nothing prevents now,' cried Roscelin triumphantly. 'I may approach her, I may lawfully ask for her, there is no barrier now. We've done no wrong, there's no shadow over us, no ban between us. I'll go and bring her home. She'll come, blithely she'll come! I knew,' he exulted, his blue eyes brilliant with vindicated joy, 'I knew we did no wrong in loving, never, never! It was *you* persuaded me I sinned. Sir, let me go and fetch her home!'

At that de Perronet took fire in his turn, with a hiss like a sulphur match flaring, and took two rapid strides foward to confront the boy. 'You leap too soon and too far, my friend! Your rights are no better than mine. I do not withdraw my suit, I urge it, I will pursue it with my might.'

'And so you may,' exulted Roscelin, too drunk with relief and delight to be ungenerous or take offence. 'I don't grudge any man his say, but on fair terms now, you and I and any who come, and we shall see what Helisende replies.' But he knew what her reply would be, his very certainty was offence, though it meant none, and de Perronet had his hand on his dagger and hotter words mounting in his throat when Audemar smote the table and bellowed them both into silence.

'Hush your noise! Am I overlord here, or no? The girl is not without kin, for she is niece to *me*. If there is anyone here who has rights in her and a duty towards her – any who has not farmed out both upon another man long since! – it is I, and I say that if Cenred so wishes, then I place her here in his fosterage, with all the rights he has exercised as her kinsman all these years. And in the matter of her marriage both he and I will take good care what is best for her, but never against her will. But now, let her be! She has asked for time untroubled, and she shall have it. When she is ready to return, I will fetch her home.'

'Content!' said Cenred, breathing deeply. 'I am content! I could ask no better.'

'And Brother . . .' Audemar turned to Cadfael. He had the entire issue in his hands now, over all matters here his writ ran, and what he ordained would be done. The least damage was his design, as his mother's had been the ultimate destruction. 'Brother, if you are going back to Farewell, tell them there what I have said. What's done is done, all that waits to be done shall be in daylight, openly. Roscelin,' he ordered sharply, turning on the boy restless and glittering with the joy of his release, 'have the horses readied, we ride for Elford. You are still in my service until I please to dismiss you, and I have not forgotten that you went forth without leave. Let me have no further cause for displeasure.'

But his voice was dry, and neither words nor look cast the least shadow upon Roscelin's exultant brightness. He bent his knee in the briefest of reverences by way of acknowledging the order, and went blithely to do his lord's bidding. The wind of his flight swung the curtain at the door, and sent a current of outer air floating across the chamber like a sigh.

Audemar looked last and longest at Adelais, who stood with eyes steady and dark upon his face, waiting his judgement.

'Madam, you will ride back with me to Elford. You have done what you came here to do.'

Nevertheless, it was Cadfael who got to horse first. No one was any longer in need of him here, and whatever natural curiosity he might feel concerning the family adjustments still to be made, and perhaps less easily accomplished than decreed, must be for ever contained, since he was unlikely to pass this way again. He reclaimed his horse without haste, and mounted, and was ambling towards the gate when Roscelin broke away from the grooms who were busy saddling Audemar's horses, and came running to his stirrup.

'Brother Cadfael . . .' He was lost for a moment for words, since his wonder and happiness were beyond words, and shook his head and laughed over his own incoherence. 'Tell her! Tell her we're free, we need not change, there's no one can blacken us now . . .'

'Son,' said Cadfael heartily, 'by this time she knows it as well as you.'

'And tell her soon, very soon, I shall come for her. Oh, yes, I know,' he said confidently, seeing Cadfael's raised brows, 'but it's me he'll send. I know him! He'd rather a kinsman he knows and can rely on, his own man, with lands bordering his own, than any lordling from distant parts. And my father won't stand between us now. Why should he, when it solves everything? What's changed, except what needed changing?'

And there was something in that, Cadfael reflected, looking down from the saddle into the young, ardent face. What was changed was the replacement of falsity by truth, and however hard the assimilation might be, it must be for the better. Truth can be costly, but in the end it never falls short of value for the price paid.

'And tell him,' said Roscelin earnestly, 'the lame brother . . . her father . . .' His voice hung on the word with wonder and awe. 'Tell him I'm glad, say I owe him more than ever can be repaid. And tell him he need never fret for her happiness, for I'll give my life to it.'

Chapter Fourteen

T ABOUT the same time that Cadfael dismounted in the court of Farewell, Adelais de Clary sat with her son in his private chamber at Elford. There had been a long and heavy silence between them. The afternoon was drawing to its close, the light dimming, and he had sent for no candles.

'There is a matter,' he said at length, stirring out of his mourne stillness, 'which has hardly been touched on yet. It was to you, madam, that the old woman came. And you sent her away with a short answer. To her death! Was that at your orders?'

Without passion she said: 'No!'

'I will not ask what you know of it. To what end? She is dead. But I do not like your manner of dealing, and I choose to have no more ado with it. Tomorrow, madam, you shall return to Hales. Hales you may have for your hermitage. But do not come back to this house, ever, for you will not be admitted. The doors of every manor of mine except Hales are henceforth closed to you.'

Indifferently she said: 'As you will, it is all one to me. I need only a little space, and may not need it long. Hales will do very well.'

'Then, madam, take your leave when you will. You shall have a safe escort on the road, seeing,' he said with bitter meaning, 'that you have parted with your own grooms. And a litter, if you prefer to hide your face. Let it not be said that I left you to travel defenceless, like an old woman venturing out alone by night.'

Adelais rose from her stool and went out from him without a word.

In the hall the servants had begun to kindle the first torches and set them in their sconces, but in every corner, and in the smoky beams of the lofty roof, darkness gathered and clung, draped cobwebs of shadow.

Roscelin was standing over the central fire on its flagged hearth, driving the heel of his boot into it to tease it into life after the damped-down hours of the day. He still had Audemar's cloak over his arm, the capuchon dangling from one hand. The light from the reviving flames gilded his stooping face into gold, smooth-cheeked, with elegant bones and a brow as fair as a girl's, and on his dreaming lips the softest and most beguiling of smiles bore witness to his deep happiness. His flaxen hair swung against his cheek, and parted above the suave nape of his neck, the most revealing beauty of the young. For a moment she stood apart in the shadows to watch him, herself unnoticed, for the pleasure and the pain of experiencing again the irresistible attraction, the unbearable bliss and anguish of beholding beauty and youth pass by and depart. Too sharp and sweet a reminder of things ended long ago, and for years believed forgotten, only to burn up into new life, like the phoenix, when a door opened, and confronted her with the ruin the years had left of the beloved being.

She passed by silently, so that he should not hear, and turn upon her the too radiant, too exultant blue eyes. The dark eyes that she remembered, deeply and delicately set beneath arched black brows, had never looked so, never for her. Always dutiful, always wary, often lowered in her presence.

Adelais went out into the chill of the evening, and turned towards her own apartments. Well, it was over. The fire was ashes. She would never see him again.

'Yes, I have seen her,' said Brother Haluin. 'Yes, I have spoken with her. I have touched her hand, it is warm flesh, woman's flesh, no illusion. The portress brought me into her presence all unprepared, I could neither speak nor move. She had been so long dead to me. Even that glimpse I had of her in the garth among the birds . . . Afterwards, when you were gone, I could not be sure I had not dreamed it. But to touch her, to have her call me by my name . . . And she was glad . . .

'Her case was not as mine, though God knows I would not say her burden has been any lighter. But she knew I was man alive, she knew where I was, and what I was, and for her there was no guilt, she had done no wrong but in loving me. And she could speak. Such words she offered me, Cadfael! 'Here is one,' she said, 'who has already embraced you, with good right. Now with good right embrace her. She is your daughter.' Can you conceive such a miracle? Giving the child to me by the hand she said it. Helisende, my daughter – not dead! Alive and young and kind and fresh as a flower. And I thought I had destroyed her, destroyed them both! Of her own sweet will the child kissed me. Even if it was only from pity – it must have been pity, how could she love one she never knew? – but even if it was only from pity, it was a gift beyond gold.

'And she will be happy. She can love as it best pleases her, and marry where her heart is. Once she called me 'Father', but I think it was as a priest, as first she knew me. Even so it was good to hear and will be sweet to remember.

'This hour we three have had together repays all the

eighteen years, even though there was so little said between us. The heart could hold no more. She is gone to her duties now, Bertrade. So must I to mine, soon . . . very soon . . . tomorrow . . .'

Cadfael had sat silent through the long, stumbling, eloquent monologue of his friend's revelation, broken by long pauses in which Haluin was rapt away again into a trance of wonder. Not one word of the abominable thing that had been done to him, wantonly, cruelly, that was washed clean away out of mind by the joy of its undoing, without a lingering thought of blame or forgiveness. And that was the last and most ironic judgement on Adelais de Clary.

'Shall we go to Vespers?' said Cadfael. 'The bell has gone, they'll all be in their places by now, we can creep in unnoticed.'

From their chosen dim corner in the church Cadfael scanned the young, clear faces of the sisters, and lingered long upon Sister Benedicta, who had once been Bertrade de Clary. Beside him Haluin's low, happy voice intoned the responses and prayers, but what Cadfael was hearing in his own mind was the same voice bleeding words slowly and haltingly, in the darkness of the forester's hay-loft, before dawn. There in her stall, serene, fulfilled and content, stood the woman he had tried to describe. 'She was not beautiful, as her mother was. She had not that dark radiance, but something more kindly. There was nothing dark or secret in her, but everything open and sunlit, like a flower. She was not afraid of anything – not then. She trusted everyone. She had never been betrayed – not then. Only once, and she died of it.'

But no, she had not died. And certainly at this moment, devout and dutiful, there was nothing dark or secret in her. The oval face shone serene, as she celebrated with joy the mercy of God, after years. Without any lingering regret; her contentment was without blemish. The vocation she had undertaken unblessed, and laboured at against the grain, perhaps, all these years, surely reached its true wholeness only now, in the revelation of grace. She would not have turned back now even for that first love. There was no need. There are seasons of love. Theirs had passed beyond the storms of spring and the heat of summer into the golden calm of the first autumn days, before the leaves begin to fall. Bertrade de Clary looked as Brother Haluin looked, confirmed and invulnerable in the peace of the spirit. Henceforth presence was unnecessary, and passion irrelevant. They were eased of the past, and both of them had work to do for the future, all the more eagerly and thoroughly for knowing, each of them, that the other lived and laboured in the same vineyard.

In the morning, after Prime, their farewells made, they set out on the long journey home.

The sisters were in chapter when Cadfael and Haluin took scrip and crutches and went out from the guest-hall, but the girl Helisende went with them to the gate. It seemed to Cadfael that all these faces about him had been washed clear of every shadow and every doubt, they had all of them that stunned brightness, astonished by the good that had befallen them. Now it could be seen more clearly how like were father and daughter, so many of the marks of the years having been smoothed from Haluin's face.

Helisende embraced him without words at parting, fervent but shy. However they had spent the previous day, whatever confidences had been exchanged, she could not so quickly know him of her own knowledge, only through her mother's eyes, but she knew of him that he was gentle and of pleasing person and address, and that his eruption into her life had freed her from a nightmare of guilt and loss, and she would always remember and think of him so, with pleasure and gratitude not so far distant from love. Profit enough, even if he never saw her again.

'God keep you, Father!' said Helisende.

It was the first and the last time that she gave him that title not as a priest but as a man, but it was a gift that would last him a lifetime.

They halted for the night at Hargedon, where the canons of Hampton had a grange, in a countryside slowly being recovered out of the waste that had followed the Norman settlement. Only now, after sixty years, was ploughland being resurrected out of the scrub, and an occasional hamlet being raised where tracks crossed, or rivers provided water for a mill. The comparative security offered by the presence of the canons, steward and servants had drawn others to settle close by, and there were now assarts being hewn out of the neglected woods by enterprising younger sons. But still it was sparsely populated territory, level, lonely and in the evening light melancholy. Yet with every laboured step taken westward across this mournful plain Brother Haluin's brightness increased, his pace quickened, and his colour flushed into eagerness.

From the narrow unshuttered window in the loft he looked out westward into a night full of stars. Nearer to Shrewsbury, where the hills began to heave their fleeces towards the mountains of Wales, earth and sky balanced in harmony, but here the vault above looked immense, and the earth of men suppressed and shadowy. The brilliance of the stars, the blackness of the space between, spoke of a touch of frost in the air, but promised a fine day for the morrow.

'And you never feel,' said Cadfael quietly, 'any desire to look back over your shoulder?'

'No,' said Haluin tranquilly. 'No need. There behind me all is well. All is very well. There is nothing now for me to do there, everything where I am bound. We are sister and brother now. We ask nothing more, we want for nothing more. Now I can bring a whole heart to God. I'm glad beyond measure that he cast me down, to raise me renewed to his service.'

There was a long, untroubled silence, while he continued to stare out into the clear night with a kind of bright hunger in his face. 'I left a leaf half-finished when we set out for Hales,' he said meditatively. 'I thought to be back to complete it long before this. I hope Anselm has not given it to someone else. It was a capital N for the 'Nunc Dimittis', still wanting half the colours.'

'It will be waiting for you,' Cadfael assured him.

'Aelfric is good, but he doesn't know my intent, he might overdo the gold.' His voice was soft and practical and young.

'Leave fretting,' said Cadfael. 'Possess your soul three days more in patience, and you'll have brush and pen in hand again, and get back to work. And so must I to my herbs, for the medicine cupboards will be running low by this time. Lie down, lad, and get your rest. There are more miles waiting for you tomorrow.'

A soft wind from the west blew in through the open window, and Haluin lifted his head and sniffed the air like a high-bred horse scenting his stable.

'How good it is,' he said, 'to be going home!'

205